Also by Polly Horvath

The Canning Season
Winner of the National Book Award

Everything on a Waffle
A Newbery Honor Book
A *Boston Globe–Horn Book* Award Honor Book

The Trolls
A National Book Award Finalist
A *Boston Globe–Horn Book* Award Honor Book

When the Circus Came to Town

No More Cornflakes

An Occasional Cow
with pictures by Gioia Fiammenghi

The Happy Yellow Car

THE

Happy Yellow Car

Car

POLLY HORVATH

A Sunburst Book
Farrar Straus Giroux

Distributed in Canada by Douglas & McIntyre Ltd.
Printed in the United States of America
First edition, 1994
Sunburst edition, 2004
10 9 8 7 6 5 4 3 2 1

Library of Congress Cataloging-in-Publication Data
Horvath, Polly.
    The happy yellow car / by Polly Horvath.
        p.   cm.
    Summary: During the Depression, Gunther Grunt buys a new
car with the money his wife has been saving to send their bright
twelve-year-old daughter to college, beginning a chain of events
that teaches the Grunts the value of their family.
    ISBN 0-374-42879-4 (pbk.)
    [1. Family life—Missouri—Fiction.   2. Depressions—1929—
Fiction.   3. Missouri—Fiction.]   I. Title.
PZ7.H79224Hap 1994
[Fic]—dc20

                                                      94-9850

For Emily Willa and
Rebecca Avery

The Happy Yellow Car

• **One** •

Once upon a time in the hilltops of Missouri lived a family named Grunt. There was Grant Grunt, Gunther Grunt, Gretel Grunt, Althea Finnerty Grunt (she who used all three names, as she was the first to point out), and, most important of all, Betty Grunt. She who would lift the family veil of ignorance. She, the basket in whom her mother, Althea Finnerty Grunt, put all her eggs. And, finally, Garth Grunt, who was small and easily forgotten, at least by Betty, who usually had her nose in a book and tended to trip over low objects.

Betty loved books. Books were the windows and paths and doors. Books were adventures she couldn't otherwise have, and books were decidedly the ticket out. Gunther Grunt worked for the railroad, and Althea Finnerty Grunt took in washing. The Grunts never went to movies, never went to diners, never went to dogfights, much less concerts. A good Christmas at the Grunt house was an orange and a stick of peppermint candy all round. But library books were free.

It was a lovely spring afternoon in the beginning of May. Gretel was working down at the bus station. Grant and Garth were coming slowly home from school together, waylaid by a springtime deluge of frogs (Garth) and girls in flowered dresses (Grant). Betty had an armload of new library books as she came up their hill, the last leg of the long walk home from school.

Betty looked up in time to see Aunt Lolly talking to her mother, who was hanging clothes on the line. Aunt Lolly was fat and mean, with a queer religious bent that kept breaking out unexpectedly. Sometimes, out of the blue, she would lunge at you and ask if you were saved. Betty thought of her as a rogue wave. In order to avoid her aunt, she headed into the trees, crept around behind the house, down into the crawl space beneath it where she could make her way back to the front of the house and under the porch steps from where she could see her mother through the wood slats and hear her conversation.

" 'Course," said Althea to Lolly, "I save a tiny pittance out of every bit I earn and squirrel it away in an old baking-powder can so that one day I can send Betty to college. The rest of them kids is too . . ."

"Dumb," said Lolly, unconcerned with the niceties and taking a huge bite of corn bread dripping with molasses. The molasses ran in a thick dark trickle down her dimpled, doughy chin.

"Someday," continued Althea, not stopping to correct Lolly or to take the clothespins out of her mouth, "them books Betty reads is gonna carry her beyond these hills. Someday she's gonna make our name. I always thought I would have maybe gone someplace if I hadn't married Gunther. Nothing against Gunther. He works hard."

"That's about all you can say for Gunther, ain't it?" said Lolly, contentedly swatting flies and wiping them on the back of her monstrous skirt. She was a mean shot with a fly, was Aunt Lolly.

Betty knew that Aunt Lolly never missed a chance to bad-mouth her father, who was partial to the exclamations "hrunk" and "hroo" to the exclusion of most of the other words available to an English-speaking person. But, thought Betty, this was no reason to suggest that he was limited. Besides, she thought, Aunt Lolly would probably bad-mouth Althea, too, if Althea wasn't her own husband Treacle's sister. In fact, Betty wondered if

Aunt Lolly and Althea would even speak to each other if they weren't both so fond of Treacle.

"Anyways," said Althea, "he's got a job."

Gobble, gobble, gobble, went Lolly. She had apparently decided that, rather than pick up the remaining corn-bread crumbs one by one, it was more efficient to dig her face right into the crumby, sticky plate and vacuum them down her fat, voracious throat.

"Not many can say they still got a job in this here depression," Althea went on.

Gobble, gobble, gobble. Betty stared with fascination through the porch slats, waiting for her aunt to come up for air. When she finally did, she said, "I don't know how you expect to get enough money for college. Waste of time anyhow, sending a girl to college. I got smart boys, but it's the army for them. Out of high school and, wham, I send them into the army."

"I cannot imagine," said Althea, separating the wet sheets that flapped on the line, "sending my boys anywhere when they are grown men. I can barely make them do anything as it is."

"Well, you ought to take a stick to them now and then," said Lolly. "It's just laziness on your part."

"I don't believe in it," said Althea primly. "Could you pass me that there laundry basket?" She pointed to one of the many baskets of wet laundry lined up on the grass next to Lolly.

"I got awfully sticky hands, honey," said Aunt Lolly, licking the molasses off her fat fingertips. "You haven't got any more of that corn bread, have you?"

"On the stove. Can I get you a piece?"

"I might have let you done that, but you didn't put nearly enough molasses on it last time. HRRRRRAGH," roared Lolly, while heaving her three-hundred-pound body out of the low-slung chair. "So I will do it myself. You never do put enough molasses on things. If you want something done right . . ." Aunt Lolly muttered, rolling and pitching on her trunklike legs toward the porch steps. Betty watched her approach with mounting horror. When her elephant-sized aunt reached the steps, Betty closed her eyes, unable to bear the sight of her from below, those huge ankles passing before her eyes. A fly settled on Betty's nose, and just as she started to brush it off she heard a most dreadful crunch, as though the very center of the earth had cracked, and looking up, saw in horror Lolly looking down as first one, then both, of her feet descended through the rotten wood.

Lolly, unable to see past her stomach, hadn't noticed Betty, but as her feet descended, and with them the collapse of the porch steps in front of them and an avalanche of rotten wood behind, although fortunately not *on* Betty, Lolly landed directly in front of her, and a little wood prison tumbled all around them. As flesh touched flesh, utter panic seized Lolly and she cried fit to raise the dead, which caused Althea to drop her laundry basket and race over, crying, "Oh, my heavens! If it isn't them dern porch steps!"

Betty thought this was stating the case rather mildly, as Lolly continued to bellow inarticulately.

"Well, goodness, come out of there. Come out of there," said Althea, as though this might not have occurred to Lolly yet.

"There's an animal, an *animal* down here with me," Lolly cried, her eyes bulging through the packed flesh of her face.

"No, no, it's just me," Betty tried to explain, her own position fraught with uncertainty, the means of escape having been cut off, and Lolly's huge feet only inches from her. It was, Betty imagined, much how broncobusters must feel as they are lowered into a pen with an angry animal, but the thrill was lost on her.

"Voices, voices!" yelled Lolly in dread. "It's Uncle Henry come back from the dead. There's a specter under the porch. A specter!"

"Now wait a second, Lolly, honey," said Althea, continuing to wring her hands. "Honey, I don't think it's a specter. I know that voice."

Just then, Betty shifted to avoid one of Lolly's dancing feet, and her socks, still wet from where she had splashed in a puddle, brushed against Lolly's leg.

"Oh, my Lord in heaven, it's *licking* me," she keened. "My God in heaven, it plans to *eat* me."

The idea of anything being able to down a tasty morsel like Lolly would have been too much for Betty's sobriety had the situation been less precarious.

"Aunt Lolly, it is not, that is, I am not, that is, it's me, your niece Betty."

"It's a drooling specter," went Lolly again, quite out of control by now.

"Oh hesh up, Lolly Finnerty, it's only Betty, for heaven's sake. Betty Grunt, you stop licking your aunt and come on out of there."

"I'm not licking her. My socks are wet and I'm trapped. She's collapsed the whole porch steps."

"It's eating me. It's eating me," roared Lolly, who wasn't much good in a crisis.

Althea took it all in and sighed, deciding she must take a gentle tack. "Now, Lolly, dear," she murmured, "it wouldn't eat you I'm sure. I'm sure even if it were an animal, which it weren't, being only our own dear Betty——" And here she stopped, as though something had just occurred to her. "And just what are you doing there, Betty Grunt? Were you listening to my private conversation?"

"Well, sort of. Oh, Lord, make her watch her *feet,* Ma."

"Lolly, do stand still, honey," said Althea, before bending to shout at Betty through the fallen boards. "And I suppose you heard about the secret college fund I been saving up for you all these years?"

"Yes, but it wasn't really my fault. I come here to read lots of times. I didn't know you would be telling secrets, but all the same, if I might take this opportunity to thank . . ." Betty broke off. It was hard to concentrate through Lolly's persistent shouts and moans; she hadn't stopped for a second, one scream leading right into the next in a symphony of distress. Betty began to suspect that she was, deep down, rather enjoying herself.

"Well, I really don't think . . . Lolly, would you please come out now, before Betty's college education is a moot point. Honey, just step on through."

But Lolly continued to go on about animals and specters until Althea, usually the soul of tact, said in exasperation, "Well, what would Uncle Henry come back to see you for anyhow? He never did like you."

Lolly stopped roaring and looked at Althea. "He did, too," she said. "He liked me plenty."

"Well, of course he did, honey," said Althea, horrified at the things that were flying out of her mouth. "He just thought you were a might touched is all. Oh, good heavens, there I go again. Let's just say he didn't always hold you accountable. Well anyhow, never mind Uncle Henry. How about just moving on out of there?"

Lolly wiggled. She wriggled. She strained this way and that, but she was stuck.

"It ain't no good. You're going to have to pull me out, and then, Lord forgive us, we is gonna release this demon of hell in here with me on the unsuspecting universe."

"For the hundredth time, Lolly, that ain't no demon, it's my daughter," said Althea.

Betty, thinking to herself, Oh, what the heck, moaned, "Ah oooooo," in sepulchral tones.

"That *is* you, Betty, isn't it? Just what is she doing down there, Althea Finnerty Grunt? That's what I'd like to know. Showing disrespect for the dead. 'Ah oooooo.' I'll be split and fried. I'll be larded like a roast. I'll be crimped like a pie."

"I guess a person can be under the porch steps if she's a mind to," said Althea, happy to put a lid on the culinary exclamations.

"Humph," said Lolly, unsatisfied. "Wouldn't catch my boys skulking around under houses. Oughta take a stick to your litter. To the whole lot of them. Come heave me outta here."

"Well . . ." said Althea uncertainly, because she

had little faith in her own frail ninety-nine pounds doing any good against the massive bulk of her sister-in-law. "I'll give it a try."

She put her two worn-to-the-bone hands around Lolly's fat wrist and tugged, but it was like trying to pull the sword from the stone.

What we need, thought Betty dispiritedly, is an incipient king.

None materialized, but she heard her brothers coming up the hill, shouting farewell insults to their friends as, reflected Betty, is the nature of boys, the little skunks.

"Now, Grant," called Althea in her reedy voice, "you just come on up this hill and pull your aunt out of the rubble."

"It's always me, it's always me," grumbled Grant. "Why don't you ever ask Garth?"

"Oh, Garth . . ." said Althea, looking at him as if she was surprised to find him there. Garth had been born a year after Althea had had twins, both of whom had died. It had been a sad time for everyone, but Althea just seemed to sleepwalk through it, and when she found herself finally with a new baby—Garth—she appeared ever after a little amazed by his existence. "Well, come on, both of you to one arm and me to the other ought to do it."

There was the sound of much labored breathing, and Betty moved frantically left to right to avoid the excited pattering feet of her aunt as she tried to tap-dance her way out of the dilemma, to no avail.

"Well, I just don't know what we are going to do," said Althea, wiping her hands off on her apron and surveying Lolly as one might a building sight.

"We could wire her and use her as a lamppost," said Grant.

"Take a stick to him!" shouted Lolly.

"Grant," said Althea reprovingly, but without as much conviction as one might expect.

"Ma, we got a baseball game," said Garth.

"All right, all right. You go on. It ain't doin' any good anyhow. We'll have to think of something else."

Betty heard the boys' feet scurry back down the hill.

"Now, Lolly," said Althea, "I don't want you takin' no offense, honey, but this puts me in mind of a greased-pig contest. I'm just gonna smear you with a little lard, honey."

Lolly set her fat lips and sulked.

"I'm sure this ain't comfortable, but you just, well, try to, well, relax," said Althea, edging away and hoping to mollify her. One did not like to be on the wrong side of Lolly Finnerty, even when she was trapped.

When Althea came back she had the lard bucket in hand, but she was finally defeated by logistics. Did one smear lard on one's sister-in-law's clothes or on her bare stomach? Althea stood and looked awkwardly at Lolly's massive stomach, until Lolly shouted, "Lord in heaven, quit standing there staring like you've been poleaxed, and hand me that there lard bucket." But Lolly, faced with a fresh housedress and a bucket of lard, wasn't sure what to do either.

"Humph!" she said, dropping the bucket. "You know whose fault this is, don't you? That no-account husband of yours, who don't even keep his home under repair."

"Now, Lolly, you know Gunther's mighty busy down at the railroad."

"Oh Lord, I pray and beseech you to get me out of the rotted trappings of this trashy family's porch steps and spare me my flesh. Amen. I hope you're praying with me, Althea Finnerty Grunt," said Lolly.

"Booo!" shouted Althea.

Underneath the porch steps Betty jumped.

"Have you gone and lost your mind?" asked Lolly.

"Well, I did think maybe I could scare you out," said Althea timidly.

"Althea Finnerty Grunt, that only works for hiccups."

"So it seems," said Althea, and went back to wringing her hands. "Lolly, honey, I don't want you to think I am blind to your plight or that of poor Betty, but, honey, I gotta finish gettin' this laundry on the line and supper made all the same. If I have an idea, I will surely let you know." Althea went back to hanging the laundry and then, when she was finished, delicately chinned herself up by the porch railing and went on into the house to make dinner.

As you can imagine, it was a terrible two hours for Betty, trapped under the steps. If only, she thought, she had her confreres, who fell down wells, with whom to compare notes. Fortunately, she had her stack of new library books to read, although it was difficult to concentrate while listening to Lolly's stream of muttered prayer and household hints. For a second, Betty had a horrible vision of Lolly with her own radio show.

Finally, when despair began to gather like black clouds, Betty heard a sound. A rumble and roar. Lolly gave a shout, and Althea came running onto the porch. The rumbling stopped and Althea gasped, "Gunther Grunt, whatever in the world!"

A hush followed. Then Lolly's huge bulk rocked from side to side and up and down, and with a crash she moved forward, broke her way through rotten timbers, and started walking down the hill on her monstrous legs, saying, "Gunther Grunt, where in tarnation did you get yourself that yeller car?"

· Two ·

Betty poked her head out and looked around. Halfway down the hill her father was standing next to the biggest, yellowest, shiniest car she had ever seen. It was a sight so extraordinary that it knocked the wind right out of her sails, and she sank back against the rotting ruins of the porch in a sort of stupor. Althea and Lolly were likewise stunned, although it hadn't affected Lolly's vocal chords.

"Gunther Grunt," she said, "you haven't answered my question. Where did the likes of you ever get a car?"

Gunther turned and leveled her a look from beneath furry eyebrows drawn in their perpetual frown. It was a look that said everything between them. It was a look that said, If I should choose to answer, it's because I feel like it and not because you deserve it.

"I bought it," he said, savoring each syllable. He trudged on up until he got to the porch. "Who broke the porch steps?" He took the laundry basket off the chair in the yard, hauled it over to the side of the porch, and stepped nimbly from it to the porch side, swinging his long legs over the porch railing.

Althea fussed behind him, crawling under rather than over the porch railing. "Oh well, it was only Lolly, and you know how rotten them porch steps were, Gunther. I guess we'll just have to have new ones. Betty, you climb out of there and help me get supper on the table."

"Bought it?" cackled Lolly. "What'd he do, rob a bank?" And shaking her head, she lumbered thunderously the rest of the way down the hill toward her own house.

Betty gathered her library books, climbed up onto the porch, and went into the house to set the table and dish out the fried apple pieces and sausages. The boys skidded in, washed their hands, and sat down. Dinner was quiet. They all wanted to know where Gunther had gotten the car, but no one dared to ask. The more tired and oil spattered he was at the end of the day, the less one wanted to appear to be questioning his judgment.

"How was the railroad?" asked Althea, timorously putting more apples on Gunther's plate. Betty watched with fascinated horror as her father sucked them up with loud slurping noises.

"Hrunk," he said. He didn't bother to cut his sausage links but put them whole into his great grinding jaws. Then he poured half a pitcher of molasses over a little corn-bread tower he had made on his plate and shoveled it in in great gulps.

Althea swabbed delicately at her mouth with her napkin during these performances and looked the other way. Suddenly, Gunther smiled to himself and said, "Hroo!"

"What's gotten into him?" whispered Grant to Garth.

"What's that, boy? You whisperin' at the table?" roared Gunther, who seemed oddly selective when it came to table manners.

"I just said you seem kind of . . . uh . . ."

"Ebullient," said Betty.

"Let the boy speak for himself," said Gunther, who didn't know what "ebullient" meant.

"You seem kind of excited," said Grant.

"OH, I DO, DO I?" said Gunther. "Hrunk, hrunk, hrunk. Dessert."

Althea put an apple pandowdy on the table.

Betty liked apples quite a bit herself, but sometimes wished there was a greater variety of fruit around.

"I wish I had a pomegranate," she said.

"Don't go givin' yourself airs," said Gunther.

"A pomegranate," said Althea. "And how the very word brings to mind a poem."

"What poem?" asked Betty.

"Don't get Ma started," whispered Grant, and kicked Betty under the table.

"ARE YOU KIDS WHISPERIN' AGAIN?" barked Gunther. "What's this, a barnyard?"

"A pomegranate is such a lovely word that it ought to have a poem written about it," said Althea, looking meaningfully at Betty. Althea just knew that Betty was awash in finer feelings, and was always most helpful in finding ways for Betty to bring them forth.

"Hrunk," said Gunther, getting up, picking up the newspaper he had brought home, and settling down next to the radio, where he was soon fast asleep. Betty cleared the table and boiled water in the kettle to wash the dishes. Gretel came home from her job at the bus station, and Althea set out the dinner she had kept hot for her, then sat down in a rocker with her mending.

"You wouldn't believe the sneaking, nasty minds of folks in a bus station if you don't give them the just exact right change. Anyone would think they thought I was doin' it on purpose," said

Gretel, chewing thoughtfully on a sausage and mulling over mankind's little peculiarities. "And you'll never guess what I saw today. Lady with triplets."

"Well, aren't you at all curious about the yellow car on the hill?" asked Grant from where he was rolling marbles.

"Now, now," said Althea nervously.

"She was struggling to carry them, all three of them, and she didn't have no baby buggy or nothin'. This depression is a terrible thing. Probably has to carry them tykes everywhere. But she was doin' it. Anyhow, she bought a ticket to Phoenix."

"Where's that?" asked Garth.

"I can't believe you aren't even *interested*," said Grant to Gretel.

"Arizona," said Gretel.

"I wonder if she was gonna have to carry those three babes in her lap the whole way," said Althea. "I wonder what she was gonna do there. It sure would make a good story. Don't you think it would make a good story, Betty?"

"Well, for heaven's sake, it's *my* story," said Gretel, giving her mother an irritated look. "And what do you think? She bought a one-way ticket."

"Leaving her husband?" asked Althea.

"If she had one. 'Course, she could be joining him there. Naturally, I couldn't ask her. Wouldn't be professional to pry into people's lives like that."

"The professional ethics of ticket sellers," said Grant, and snorted.

"It's a slice of life down there at the bus station. Okay, who parked the car on our hill?" asked Gretel.

"Pa!" said Grant and Garth, and enjoyed her reaction.

"What's Pa doing with a car?" whispered Gretel.

"Nobody knows," said Grant, making his voice mysterious.

"Children, time for bed," said Althea, and shooed them upstairs.

Betty went to her room and put her hair in a scarf to try to make it lie flat, which, she hoped, would make her round face look thinner. Then she took a book and lay in bed, watching Gretel go through her closet and criticize all her clothes before selecting the least despicable dress to wear to work the next day. Soon Gretel, worn out with the slices of life, was snoring quietly in bed. Betty couldn't sleep. A college education! She had always known she was destined for greatness, but a college education besides! She crept out of bed and leaned out the window, looking down the hill to the yellow car shining in the moonlight. Suddenly, she heard a cry. Leaning a bit farther, she could see her parents sitting in two of the rockers on the porch. Her mother was clutching something in her hands.

"Gunther Grunt," she said. "Did you take the money from this baking-powder can?"

"Now, that ain't no place to keep money, Althea," said Gunther, his bushy eyebrows, usually drawn into a terrible frown, now arched guiltily over his shifting eyes. Betty climbed out the window onto the steep pitch of the roof and scooted down the side of it until she was squatting within easy sight and sound of her parents. She banked on them not looking upward, since few people do during intense discussions.

"Have you seen it, Gunther? Did you take it, Gunther? I was savin' that money for Betty's college education."

"Oh, hrunk," said Gunther. "What is she gonna do with a college education anyhow? She's probably gonna be married and that way before she's old enough to go to college."

"What happened to my money, Gunther?" asked Althea, not to be deflected.

"Well, I like that. *Your* money. Money to feed this family, that's what it is."

"Where is it, Gunther? I had almost eighty dollars saved. I been savin' since she was four and taught herself to read. If you got a child who's specially smart, you gotta do right by them. I been takin' in extra, yes *extra,* washing—over and above what I could do with any ease—and putting that money away. So now, you tell me where my money is."

"Well, it's kind of a funny thing you mentioning it, 'cause I just happened to find it last week. You sure can keep a secret, Althea, I'll say that for you."

"Did you put it in the bank?"

"Well, I thought of it, but I ain't got much use for banks after I seen what can happen to them. But it seemed to me there must be a better place for that money than that there baking-powder can. You don't want someone coming and stealing it, now, do you? I had it in my wallet and I guess I kind of forgot about it, and it's a good thing, because today, hrunk, hrunk, you won't believe it. This lady, I'm walkin' to work and goin' by where Hank has his car lot, and she comes up. She's an old lady but she looks like an old *rich* lady, and she says, 'Mister, you wanna buy a car? It ain't hardly been driven, and my husband has passed on and can't drive it no more, so I am gonna sell it.' 'Well,' I say, 'I'm just lookin', I'm just admirin', I ain't got money for a car.' She says, 'Give you a good deal.' So I say, 'How much?' and she says, 'Eighty bucks.' Well, it was the eighty bucks that kind of got to me. She wants to sell me a car for the *exact* same amount of money I got in my wallet. Seemed like it was kind of ordained to me. You know, like by a higher being."

"Gunther Grunt, don't blaspheme!" said Althea in shocked tones.

"I didn't mean *the* higher being. Just maybe one

or other of them archangels. So she takes me over to her house, and she's got this big house—pillars, stuff like that—and this yeller car sitting in the driveway. So I bought it. I was almost late for work."

"You bought a car," hissed Althea. Betty had never heard her mother hiss before, and she almost fell off the roof. "You bought a car with Betty's college-education money? We don't have enough money for *gas*. Where did you plan on going with this car of yours, Gunther?"

"This lady, she put some gas in the car for me," said Gunther, looking down at his feet.

"Do you expect the gas to last forever?" Althea said.

"Hrunk," said Gunther.

"I don't know what to say, Gunther Grunt. I truly don't," said Althea.

"Look at it," said Gunther. "Shinin' in the moonlight."

"All I see is Betty's college-education fund," said Althea, standing up and rallying. "On four wheels!" And she went in the house, slamming the door behind her.

Betty scooted backward up the roof and climbed in her window. She lay shivering in bed, pulling the moth-eaten wool blanket tighter around her. How nice to be like Gretel, able to sleep through anything. She hated it when her parents fought and the cold silence lay like snow around the house afterward. She wanted to wake up Gretel and tell her about it, but she knew Gretel would, first of all, shrug off the fight and, second, demand to know why Betty got all the college-education funds around here. Betty got up and leaned out the window again. Her father was sitting on the porch just staring at the car.

· Three ·

The next morning was a flurry of activity as usual, with lunch packing and book sorting. Gunther and Gretel had already left for work, so Grant dared to ask his mother if they could get in the car just to see what the inside was like.

"What car would that be?" asked Althea, washing off the kitchen table.

"Well, heck, how many cars does this family have?" asked Grant.

"Don't you speak to your mother that way, Grant," said Althea.

"He means the yellow car, Ma," said Garth.

"Oh, Garth . . ." said Althea.

"THE YELLOW CAR!" shouted Grant.

"I don't know what vehicle about which you speak," said Althea with great formality. "Now you go on to school. Go on, now. Land's sake, if this family is gonna get an education, I can see it's gonna be up to me."

The children ran out. When they got as far as the car, Grant shushed them and squatted behind it. He peeked out. "She's not looking," he said. "Let's get in."

They got in and admired the soft gold seats and shiny interior.

"How'd Pa ever get the money for something like this? Whew!" said Grant.

"My college-education fund," said Betty.

"Your what?"

"Ma's been saving up for my college education on account of I'm so smart," said Betty, unable to resist this dig.

"Huh," said Grant wittily. "Who wants to go to college anyhow?"

"You needn't worry, no one's going to force *you*," said Betty sweetly.

"Looks to me," said Grant, pointedly patting the soft interior of the car, "like it's not something you're going to have to fret over either."

He laughed a nasty laugh. Betty hit him with her lunch pail, and a fight would have erupted, but Garth said, "Run! Ma's comin' with some laundry."

The children rolled out and down the springtime hill and ran along the road. Grant's school was several blocks past Betty and Garth's, so, although they started out together, he often left them behind to eat his dust. When Betty got to the door of her school, her best friend, Almira Poofpoff, came racing up to her.

"Oh Betty, you'll never believe it. You'll just never believe it! You've been elected the Willowdale School's annual Pork-Fry Queen!" said Almira happily. Every May the Willowdale's two sixth-grade classes voted one of the sixth graders to be the Pork-Fry Queen at the big June Festival and Barbecue.

"Me? The Pork-Fry Queen?" exclaimed Betty, astonished. Her first thought was, It must be my hair. She knew she was popular with the other children. She was always cheerful and friendly, always ready to help those of lesser intelligence with their homework. A smile and a wave for everyone, that was her. But to be Pork-Fry Queen one needed more than this, one needed good hair. She figured the scarf had done its trick. Betty's head, left to its own devices, resembled a dust ball. Her hair wouldn't lie flat and sleek in the manner of intellectual hair the world over. No, it had the fluffy mass of the bird-brain. This, combined with her chipmunk cheeks, made her rather less the beauty-queen type and more the rodent-gathering-nuts-for-winter type.

"I may not be pretty but I'm Pork-Fry Queen," Betty said, reading the notice on the bulletin board. She repeated this over and over to herself all afternoon, each time reveling in the rush of glory she felt. Here was concrete proof that virtue was rewarded. It hardly seemed possible to her, even though it was right there on the bulletin board. She waited for Miss Fenster to announce it in class, but Miss Fenster was strangely quiet.

"Betty, can you stay a minute," called Miss Fenster as the class got up to leave at the end of the day.

When everyone had left, Miss Fenster stacked her papers slowly and deliberately on her desk before addressing Betty.

"Now, Betty, as I'm sure you know, you've been elected this year's Pork-Fry Queen."

"Yes, ma'am," said Betty.

"This is, as you know, a not inconsiderate honor," continued Miss Fenster.

Betty winced but kept quiet. Miss Fenster's speech was sprinkled heavily with near hits.

"By secret ballot fair and square; though I must say, I personally counted the ballots twice, because Janine Woodrow received quite a few votes, too."

Betty sighed. Janine Woodrow's parents owned the only department store in town. Janine had long golden hair. She had two pairs of school shoes and a pair of party shoes that her mother let her wear to school. And she had a seemingly endless supply of crisply pleated plaid skirts and fresh white blouses that Betty had spent the last few years lusting after. Betty's mother made all her dresses and Betty despised them.

"Janine would, ahem, fit into the Pork-Fry Queen dress without"—and here Miss Fenster gave her a long critical look—"any alterations at all."

Betty blushed. Miss Fenster was staring rudely at her stocky figure and noticeably comparing her to Janine.

"Your mother, of course, will have to make the necessary adjustments. We're not set up for that kind of thing here. I myself do not sew. I went to college rather than learn the domestic arts."

"I'm going to college someday," said Betty, so uplifted with her grand news that she was willing to try to establish a fellow feeling between herself and Miss Fenster, known in some circles as Miss Fenster the Dumpster.

"We shall see," said Miss Fenster, sniffing. "At any rate, I just wish to remind you of a few salacious points. Point number one, we expect our Pork-Fry Queens to be spotless in word and deed. No spitballs on the playground, no cheating on tests."

"I promise," said Betty, who never spat or cheated.

"Keep your chin clean and your standards high."

Betty nodded mutely.

"And you'll have to come up with a dollar for flowers by the end of the month. The Pork-Fry Queen always supplies her own flowers."

Here was the fly in the ointment.

"We've got flowers all over our hill, Miss Fenster. I know my brothers and I could pick some. We could pick lots."

"Wildflowers," said Miss Fenster, "would not be suitable. You may go."

"Yes, ma'am," said Betty, and slunk out. Where was she ever going to get a dollar for flowers? On the other hand, mayhaps there were some stray quarters lurking in a baking-powder can somewhere. She ran home.

Her mother was standing next to a line of laundry baskets, bending, clipping, bending, clipping. As Betty approached, she heard Althea muttering to herself.

Her mother turned around and said, "Oh, Betty, here I am yammering away to myself like a woman possessed. I'm just so mad at the sinful way some people waste money we don't have. Well, never mind."

Betty had been all set to tell her mother about the Pork-Fry honor, but now she wasn't sure it was a good idea. "Ma, suppose that Gretel wanted to be a beauty queen, would you give her a dollar?" she asked, casually putting down her books and helping her mother hang up clothes.

"Betty Grunt, you know I haven't got a spare nickel, let alone a dollar."

"I thought you put away a little extra money in a baking-powder can."

"Well, that money's all spent now, ain't it?" said her mother bitterly. "And besides, it was hard enough to put that money away, working year after year. But it's one thing to put it away for college and another thing to go frittering it away on beauty queens and the like. Believe me, honey, the beauty queens of this world never amount to anything in the long run. After their day in the sun, they go straight to gin and rented rooms and dissipation, until finally they end up playing the tuba in the Salvation Army band."

Betty tried to imagine Janine Woodrow playing the tuba.

"And what is all this about Gretel being a beauty queen, anyhow?" asked her mother, putting her hands on her hips and staring down at Betty.

"She's not, she's not," said Betty quickly. "I just said what if."

"Well, what if your grandmother had wheels, she'd be a bicycle. Haven't you got anything better to do than bother your mother with what ifs. Now, go get yourself some rock cookies and do your homework."

Betty picked up her books, went in, grabbed a handful of walnut and raisin cookies, and went out to the orchard, where she vented her frustration by running up and down the rows of budding trees, arms akimbo, screaming *"Heathcliff! Heathcliff!"* But even this was small balm to her heavy heart. When she had done her homework and dinnertime seemed imminent, she plodded back to the house, where she found her parents in the middle of the continuing battle.

"I'm tellin' you, we is all goin' for a drive this Sunday and that's why I bought the gloves. You ain't the only one with a baking-powder can."

"Well, my gosh, Gunther, a drive in what?"

"The car, the car, darn you."

"Don't say 'darn' to me, Gunther Horatio Grunt. And I do not know the vehicle of which you speak."

"Gol darn it, Althea. How can you be so pig-headed? The car is bought and paid for. You might as well ride in it."

"I'm going to dish up dinner now, Gunther," said Althea.

Gunther stamped his foot, muttered to himself, and went inside to wash the oil off his hands. At dinnertime, after grace, Gunther completed his amazing two-day performance by handing out dainty white gloves.

"Are we goin' to a cotillion, Gunther?" asked

Althea, and put her gloves gently back in their box.

"The gloves," said Gunther, ignoring her, "are for riding in the car and only for riding in the car. We are goin' to go for a family drive. That's what rich folk do. They go for a family drive on Sunday, and this family is doin' the same. We may be rail-roaders, but we got as much yeller car as anyone and we are goin' to use it. Now the first one I catch entering that car without lily-white gloves on his hands is gonna wish he hadn't've, do I make myself clear?"

The children looked at their sparkling white gloves and nodded their heads.

"I don't wanna wear gloves," ventured Garth tentatively, after they had all eaten in silence a few minutes.

"They had a sale on these here gloves, so these here gloves are what we are wearin'," said Gunther between mouthfuls.

"But, Pa," said Garth.

"Shut up," said Gunther, and that was that.

After dinner, when Gretel had come in and shared her slice of life with them, Betty took her aside and said, "Do you ever save out any of the money you make, or do you give it all to Ma and Pa?"

"What's it to you?" whispered Gretel.

"I need some money," said Betty.

"For what?" asked Gretel incredulously.

"I've been voted the Pork-Fry Queen."

"Feh," said Gretel, ever the sympathetic ear. Ever the soul of kindness. "Don't bother me with your sixth-grade doings."

"I need that money, Gretel."

"So, what if you do? What's it to me?"

"Couldn't you lend me a dollar?"

"A dollar? What do you think I'm made of, money? I keep back a penny here, a penny there when I baby-sit or something extra on the side, but don't you think Pa keeps track of what I earn and what I spend? You know how hard it is to put aside enough for lipstick? You think I got a dollar to give you?"

"Lend," amended Betty.

"Go away, and stop bothering me," said Gretel wearily, and went to boil some water to wash her hair. Betty did the dishes slowly and contemplatively. Her father rocked in the corner by the radio, and her mother picked up the never-ending mending. Betty leaned over the sink tiredly. "Down," she muttered, "but not out."

Betty spent all day Saturday up in her favorite apple tree, enjoying the blossoms and eating last year's apples and watching the clouds float by, trying to think of a way to earn a dollar in time to be crowned Pork-Fry Queen. She could think of lots of ways to earn the money, but was impeded by that old bugaboo, age. Who would hire a twelve-year-old, no matter how brilliant and charming? However, being full of hope, the high spirits of youth, and lots of fructose, she swung happily from the apple boughs, deciding to put the squeeze on her brothers.

At supper she sat next to Grant. She passed him the corn bread and pork fat. She let him take the drumstick and gnawed on a wing, even though it was her and Garth's turn for a drumstick. When he spilled milk on her, she batted her baby browns and said, "How clumsy of me. I must have jogged your elbow."

Grant ignored her throughout, but Betty hoped a little of her charity and sisterly devotion was soaking through his crusty exterior and draining into his ooshy mellow undering. It was Betty's contention that everyone, even her father, had beneath his protective crust an ooshy mellow undering. One didn't necessarily want to see it, any more than one wanted to see one's guts prominently displayed; it was enough to know it existed. Therefore, she was somewhat disappointed to find that bringing more pie and milk to Grant, as he sat listening to the radio and feigning a deep and abiding interest in Jack Armstrong (hero to all American boys), did nothing to melt his heart.

"I'm going to Larry's," he said as he got his jacket on. "Oh," he added, picking up his cap and walking out the door, "and, Betty, whatever it was you thunk you was gonna get out of me, you can just forget it."

"I didn't thunk nothing," said Betty sourly. "How can anyone, even *you,* reach the age of fourteen and still think there's such a word as *thunk?*" she shouted at his retreating back.

"Now, Betty, dear," said Althea, darning a sock, "he don't have your advantages. You been reading since you were four, but he don't have your and mine vocabulary."

Her mother had switched radio stations and was now listening peacefully to some violin music instead of to Jack Armstrong. Gunther was on the porch looking at the car.

Gretel came in and inhaled her dinner. She had no time for a slice of life tonight. On Saturday nights she ran home from work, ate dinner, changed into her Saturday night dress, and caught the bus back to town with her two girlfriends, who also worked in town. They went to movies and didn't come in until late at night. Betty envied Gretel these mad adventures and longed to hear about them, but Gretel refused to volunteer any information.

"You is too young and innocent," she chortled merrily, setting her hat on at different angles.

"Well, you better not get in too late tonight. Tomorrow's a big day," said Betty, lying on her stomach on her bed and surveying Gretel's preparations critically. "I like it better the first way. That way just looks affected."

"You think? I ain't coming in early from the only fun I ever have."

"Well, it's my first car ride and I plan to get a good night's sleep," said Betty.

"I suppose Pa is going to make us all sit like sardines in that car and probably drive us off a cliff. Did it ever occur to anyone that Pa hasn't never driven a car before?"

"He drove it home."

"I guess he must have, but it's a wonder to me that he arrived in one piece. I could drive the dern car. I know how but don't suppose he'll ever let me. Leastways we'd all be safe."

"How'd you learn to drive? I didn't think you'd ever been in a car before," said Betty.

"What you don't know would fill one of them books of yours," said Gretel soothingly, and made kissing faces at herself in the mirror. "Don't wait up for me," she called gaily over her shoulder, and left. Betty stared at her green bedroom walls. There was no one left to ask but Garth, and it hardly seemed likely that Garth would have any money. The only money she had ever known him to have was a nickel he got once for rescuing a woman's dog from an oncoming train. She tried to think if he had ever spent that nickel . . .

She raced down the stairs, out the door, and around back, where he was sitting on the ground scratching out one of his cities of rocks and sticks and peopling it with the dead bugs he saved. Betty usually found this a disgusting occupation and stayed clear of it, but this evening she sat dejectedly in the dirt beside him and tried to look interested.

"Why, what a nice little city," she said sweetly.

Garth looked up at her as though he couldn't quite believe his eyes. His face was smeared with dirt from where he had wiped a filthy hand under his running nose. His big brown eyes were like saucers in his quiet face.

"It's Motor City," he said excitedly, when he had decided that she was there to stay. "These here rocks are my cars. This is a blue one, and this is a yeller one like ours, and these are red and orange, and on race days, like today, they go racing. See, they start at the church, and they go down this lane to the school, and they hop over this dead bug who is the mayor, and they . . ."

"Garth," interrupted Betty, "how much money do you suppose you have?"

"Oh, I got a bank," said Garth, speeding the rocks around obstacles.

"You do?" asked Betty with mounting enthusiasm.

"Sure, it's behind them bushes. You want to see

it? That's the other part of Motor City. It's got a bank and a soda fountain and a swimming pool."

"Oh," said Betty. "I don't suppose you have any *real* money in that bank?"

"Sure, these folks gotta keep their money there. 'Cause if you keep your money in cans, other folks take it."

Betty wondered whether the whole family sat around of an evening listening at windows.

"Garth," she began again, "can we just forget Motor City for a minute?" She put her hand under his chin and made him look at her. He yanked her hand away and went back to digging with a stick. Betty sighed. "Garth, do you, for instance, still have that nickel that lady gave you for rescuing her dog?"

"Nope."

"What did you do with it?"

"S'my nickel," said Garth fearfully.

"I know it's your nickel. I'm just curious."

"You're not curious. You want my nickel."

"Well, for heaven's sake, you said you didn't have it anymore, so what's the difference if you tell me how you spent it?" shouted Betty in exasperation. She didn't even care now about getting the nickel. She just wanted to impress upon him the importance of telling one's sister everything.

"I bought baseball cards with it," he said.

"You don't have any baseball cards," said Betty.

"Do," said Garth. "Do, s'matter of fact."

"Well, I've never seen them, and if they were in the house, I would have." She and her mother cleaned the house from top to bottom every Sunday, and Betty took the opportunity to snoop as much as she could in everyone's drawers. She knew that Gretel had a new pair of silky blue underpants she hadn't shown anyone and that Grant had a note from his teacher telling Althea that his seeming impartiality to all subjects alike bore further scrutiny, a note that had never found its way to their mother. She knew her mother kept a bouquet of pressed dried flowers in her Bible. Betty wanted to ask her mother the story behind this, but somehow couldn't bring herself to do so. She was pretty sure that if Garth had any baseball cards she would have seen them by now.

"I don't believe you," she said.

Garth got up. "Turn your back," he said.

"Why?" asked Betty.

"Just turn it."

She revolved with a sigh and heard him go off. When he returned, he had a bag with baseball cards in it.

"You couldn't have bought all these with a nickel," she said, peering in at the pile of cards.

"Nope," said Garth, and sat back down to play in Motor City. "You can look at them if you want to," he added generously.

The last thing she cared about was a bunch of dusty baseball cards, but she feigned interest, turning them over as she thought things through. How had Garth gotten the money for them? What other secrets did he keep in his little six-year-old head?

"You see this car?" said Garth, breaking the silence. "He's gonna run right into the yeller one if it don't watch out."

"Will someone in this house please say *yellow*?" Betty barked irritably. *"Yell ow. Yell ow ow ow ow.* Not 'yeller.' It's not that hard!"

"He bumped into him all right. Now they is gonna fight," Garth continued imperturbably.

"I guess you haven't any money then," she said, and handed him his baseball cards.

He closed the bag. "Turn your back again."

She spun around. Did she care where he kept his silly baseball cards? Did she care how he had gotten them?

She waited patiently, not wanting to antagonize him. Approaching him slowly, slowly as a snake does a frog. When he had settled again in the dust, she said, "Garth, honey, suppose you tell me the truth now. Do you have some money, just a little, stashed somewhere oh so cleverly?"

"No," said Garth, picking up the mayor, who, although a dead beetle, had many important functions to attend.

"Garth, bedtime!" called Althea from the porch. Garth wiped his dusty hands on his filthy overalls and ran toward the house. Betty stared off into the thickening dusk of the orchard over which night clouds rode on the disappearing light, and thought hard.

· Four ·

The Grunts' Sunday had an unchanging agenda and rhythm. Gretel and Gunther had Sunday off from work. The children had no school. Everyone slept late, except for Althea. She rose at the cockcrow to bake eight loaves of yeast bread, which, supplemented with corn bread, would see the Grunts through the week. Next, she did the Grunts' washing, which she was unable to get to during the week due to the washing she took in. By this time, everyone was up. Then Althea and Betty began the Sunday scrub-down.

Althea hated working on Sunday, which she had been taught was a day of rest, but no matter how she tried to juggle things, it seemed there were always chores left over, so she finally decided that anyone who created the world in six days ought to forgive a little expediency. Althea and Betty took big buckets of soapy water and wire brushes and scrubbed the floors and cabinets, dusted, made beds, and generally licked the rafters clean. After that, full of virtue and a sense of accomplishment, they made and ate a big Sunday dinner and rested the remainder of the afternoon until it was time for church. The Grunts went to an evening service. Althea would have preferred a morning service, where she could have seen more of her friends, but, said Gunther, if he was going to be dragged to Jesus, he was going to do so fully awake. And that was that.

This Sunday began the same way. Betty and Althea cleaned and scrubbed as furiously as always, and Betty wondered, as her mother had not once mentioned the yellow car, if perhaps her father had given up on the idea of an elegant begloved ride. But after dinner, as soon as he had taken his dirty napkin out of his shirtfront, wiped his grease-stained fingers on the tablecloth, and belched once or twice, he said, "Go get your gloves."

The children ran to their rooms for their spotless gloves. They were dressed in their best Sunday clothes. Then they raced (all except Gretel, who sported a dissipated saunter) down to stand by the car and await further instructions. Gunther appeared wearing his own gloves, which, Betty noted, were not white, and something on his head, which she felt sure must be his idea of a driving cap. It was a funny affair that reminded her of a baseball cap; but he seemed to be under the impression that it was dashing, for he lifted his chin, and the hollows of his face became less cantankerous and more aristocratically aloof. It was, she pondered, amazing what a hat could do.

"Children, you sit in back," he said.

There was a great deal of scrambling for a window seat at first. Garth kicked Betty in the stomach once or twice as he tried to crawl over her to get to the window. Finally, their mother appeared. She had her thin, worn cloth coat wrapped tightly about her and, with a stony expression, she descended the stairs that Gunther had fixed. When she got to the car she opened the door gingerly, as if she thought it might bite, and then, pursing her lips, she settled in the front seat.

"Hrunk," said Gunther, and started the engine. He was not very good at driving. One couldn't ignore this as they veered from side to side, barely missing fences and ditches and hitting squarely every pothole and bump in the road, causing them all to bounce up and down. Fortunately, by the time they met up with other traffic toward town, he seemed to be getting the hang of it and they stayed pretty much on the road. No one had said a word up to this point. Whether they were enthralled with the experience of a car ride or too terrified to speak was hard to tell. Or perhaps they just hated to break the spell that hung over them, in their Sunday best and fresh white gloves, being squired about like Missouri aristocrats.

"Where are we going?" asked Garth, finally.

"I know where we're *not* going, we're *not* going to college," said their mother.

"I know that. Where are we going?" persisted Garth.

"A drive ain't supposed to be *to* somewhere. A drive is just a drive," barked their father with unusual chattiness.

"Well, it seems to me . . ." began Grant, but no one would ever know how it seemed to him, because at that moment there was a loud popping sound. Gretel and Althea shrieked. The car wobbled wildly and then skidded to the side of the road.

"You busted a tire," said Grant.

Gunther stopped the car and rested his forehead on the steering wheel for a second. "Hroo," he said.

"Lord in heaven! What happened? I declare my stuffings were knocked loose that time. Are you children all right?" asked Althea.

"Busted a tire," said Grant dismally.

"Are we there yet?" asked Garth.

Althea looked around. "Well, I guess we can walk home or walk to town."

"I think I'll just take a little snooze," said Gretel, leaning back against the seat and closing her eyes. "Late night."

"All we gotta do is change a tire," said Grant. Betty was surprised to find out that he seemed to know about such things. To her knowledge, he had never even been around a car before. "You got a spare tire, Pa?"

"Hrunk," said Gunther. "No jack."

"Good night," said Gretel sleepily.

"Farmhouse up there. Could be they'd lend us one," said Gunther.

Althea peered down the long dusty road at the farmhouse.

"Boys," she said to Grant and Garth, "you run ahead and knock on the door and see if they wouldn't just lend us a jack. No sense us all getting dusty in our best clothes. 'Course we wouldn't *be* ruining our best and like as not having to walk miles and miles if we'd set our sights on things like higher education." And Althea crossed her ankles and folded her hands primly in her lap, as though she was prepared to bear the slings and arrows with as much dignity as possible.

The boys shot out of the car and down the road. Betty gazed at her mother and her father's thundering brow and the gently snoring Gretel and, without asking permission, got out of the car and ran on ahead with her brothers.

"Garth?" she said when she caught up with him.

"Hmm?" he asked.

"I've been thinking. I won't ask you where you are getting money to buy baseball cards, but if you'd just lend me a dollar—that is, instead of spending it on more baseball cards—I promise I will find some way to pay you back with interest."

Grant looked at her. "Why are you pestering Garth?"

"Do *you* have a dollar?" demanded Betty.

"No," said Grant.

"Then what do *you* care?" asked Betty irritably. "How about it, Garth?"

"Don't say anything," said Grant to Garth.

"Don't listen to Grant," said Betty.

"Nuts," said Grant, and spat into the dusty road. "I won't have him taken advantage of by a bossy sister who's never shown any interest in him afore this."

"Before," said Betty.

"Oh, you think you're so smart with your college-education fund," said Grant, and spat again.

Garth looked on, big-eyed and gratified. No one had ever paid so much attention to him before. Certainly this was the first time anyone had fought over him.

"Anyhow, he's not saying anything," said Grant stubbornly.

"My lips are sealed," said Garth, delighted with himself for digging this phrase up from the dim reaches of his brain. Really, the day was getting better and better. If this kept up, perhaps he could have the whole family fighting over him.

"Come on, Garth." Grant poked Garth, and the boys started to run the last bit to the farmhouse, with Betty, never the Olympian athlete, in pursuit. She reached them just as they arrived at the door and knocked on it.

It was opened slowly, revealing a dark recess from which an evil eye and part of a beard, presumedly evil as well, appeared.

"Yeah?" came a low voice from the beard.

"Our car broke down," said Garth.

"We need a jack. Do you have one you could lend us?" asked Grant. "We see you got a truck."

The door opened a bit more. Two men loomed in the doorway, filling it. The smell of work, sweat, manure, dirt, and whiskey blasted out like an arctic air floe.

"Never mind," said Betty, edging down the steps.

"You want a jack or not? What is this, some kind of trick?" roared the second man, who was tall and bald. He looked distinctly like the giant in "Jack and the Beanstalk." Betty gaped at him. Garth quivered. Only Grant retained his savoir faire.

"No, sir, it's no trick," he said. "We need a jack all right."

"I'll get it, Sam," said the giant to the dark and hairy one, and lurched off in the direction of the truck. Suddenly, a dog lunged out and began barking at the children's ankles.

"Nice dog," said Grant, but now even his voice shook slightly.

"Don't worry," said Sam, evidently enjoying their fright to the full. "He ain't et anyone . . . yet. Hey, Mac," he called to the giant, "we better go with them to their car. Easiest thing in the world to ride off with our jack."

"We wouldn't want that to happen now, would we?" growled Mac the giant, returning with the jack.

"No, you certainly wouldn't," squeaked Betty, in what she could not help but feel were not heroic tones.

Dark and hairy Sam nodded his head in the direction of the road, and they all tramped silently down it, Garth and Betty hanging on to Grant's sleeves. When they got closer, Grant pointed and said, "There we are."

"Well, looky what we got here," said giant Mac.

"Well, looky at that. Indeedy do," said dark and hairy Sam.

"We got ourselves a car full of rich folks, wouldn't you say, Sam?"

"I'd say that, Mac."

"Well, then, I guess you'd be wrong, heh, heh, heh," said Grant. "I guess you'd maybe want to guess again."

The operative word, thought Betty, seems to be *guess*.

Dark and hairy Sam and giant Mac stood in their tracks. Mac swung the jack around his head several times in a distinctly menacing way. "Folks like you livin' off the fat of the land have ruined folks like us."

"Your daddy tell you half the country's starving 'cause of folks like you driving your fancy cars and wearing your fancy clothes?" asked dark and hairy Sam, eyeing Betty.

"You don't understand," Betty mustered through a dry mouth, her tongue suddenly sticking to her teeth.

"Oh, we don't understand, huh, sister?" said giant Mac, swinging the jack faster and faster.

"We'll see about that," began dark and hairy Sam, putting a hand on Betty's shoulder.

"You take your hands off her!" said Grant, and before Betty knew what was happening, Grant had kicked dark and hairy Sam in the shins and pulled Betty out of his surprised clutches. Betty didn't stop to figure things out but ran down the road on adrenaline-powered legs, with the pitter-patter of Garth's feet behind her. She was almost at the car before she even thought to turn around, and then she gasped. Dark and hairy Sam had hold of Grant, who was twisting this way and that. Just then, Gunther shot past Betty, with Althea not far behind, while Garth and Betty panted by the car and Gretel snored gently within it. Betty, filled with shame at her thoughtless flight down the road, walked back toward the melee and then gasped again as she saw her father take a long swing and deck dark and hairy Sam. Giant Mac looked on with a bemused expression, having abandoned his jack swinging in the excitement. Dark and hairy Sam was starting to get up as Betty neared and heard Althea say, "Well, stars above, and I never did. Samuel MacPherson, it's me!"

Dark and hairy Sam stopped and turned to Althea. A look of utter delight crossed his Neanderthal features as he exclaimed, "Althea Finnerty, as I live and breathe!"

"Finnerty Grunt now," said Althea, chortling away. "Well, Lord, who'd ever have thought? How many years has it been, Cousin Sam? Twenty? Thirty? I hate to think. Why, I'm surprised you even recognized me, my, my."

"I'd know you anywhere, Althea. I never forgot you, darlin'. Why, last time I seen you, you was giving me such a speech. How you couldn't possibly marry your own cousin, even a second cousin. How you was gonna go study up some opera in the big city. Gonna have a different life than here in the country. Gonna marry big, live rich, see the world. Maybe live in Italy. Gosh, what a kid you was!" And he slapped his knee, remembering.

Betty stared in astonishment at her mother, who was growing more and more uncomfortable. Then, for a moment, there was a far-off, wistful look in her mother's eyes that went straight to Betty's heart.

"But gol darn it, looks like you done it, too," said Sam, pointing to the car.

"What's that?" asked Althea, looking ashamed. Then she straightened. "Well, yes," she began.

"Hrunk," said Gunther, and cleared his throat.

"Now hush up, Gunther," said Althea with authority. "It's okay to go braggin' on your husband to your own kith and kin, after all. Yes, Gunther has done real well for himself in the railroadin' business. 'Course opera studyin' was fine, jest fine for a while, but you know a woman really wants to raise a family, and Gunther, he don't like me to work. Sundays, why, we just get into our oldest clothes and take a drive in one of our cars. These roads are so dusty, I declare. Not like them Italian roads. Still, it's home. We live hereabouts, too, you know. But enough about me. What are you boys doing living here? I thought you had left Missouri years ago."

Sam slapped his knees and guffawed. "If that don't beat all. Us practically neighbors and not even knowing it! We sure enough did leave. Went to work the oil fields in Oklahoma and did all right, too. Enough to buy this farm a few years back. Sad thing is, it's going belly-up now. Seems no one can hang on to their land no more. 'Course, if we had a few dollars to tide us over the crunch . . . "

"Well, let's all of us go and change that tire," said Althea. "This here is Betty, and this is Grant, and this is Garth. Gretel's asleep in the car. Deb parties and such."

While Althea kept up a constant chatter, hoping to avoid the subject of loans for needy relatives, Mac bent over and whispered to Garth and Betty, who were sitting on the side of the road, "You tell me straight, did your ma get Hilda's money? I always thought it was just a rumor. One of those things people invent to talk about in the country when they get bored enough."

"Aunt Hilda?" asked Betty, openmouthed. "What money?" She said it with such obvious incredulity that Mac straightened up and said, "Never you mind." The grownups were finishing with the tire, and everyone was shaking hands and preparing to say goodbye.

"Yes," said Sam to Gunther this time. "I sure could use a boost. Few hundred dollars make all the difference in the world to me."

"Well, heck," said Gunther, "I ain't got a plugged nickel to spare." And snorted at the very idea.

"Children, get in the car," said Althea, getting in herself. "Now, Cousin Sam, you know how it is with businessmen. Particularly in this here depression. Everything tied up. No cash. I hear prosperity's right around the corner though," she sang out as Gunther started the car. He drove down to the Macphersons' driveway and turned around.

"Well, hey, where you all live?" called Sam, as the car passed them trudging back to the farmhouse on their return trip.

"Be good to yourselves, boys!" called Althea gaily.

They traveled in silence. The children were not at all sure what to make of their mother's little holiday from honesty.

"Ma," Betty finally ventured timidly.

"Now you just hush up. I'm sure Mac and Sam knew I was only kidding. I know them far better than you children do, and I'm sure they did. Anyhow, if I want to be rich for one day in my life, well, I expect I have every right to be. Anyhow, I'm sure I could have been an opera singer if I'd have had a mind to." And Althea fell to singing little snatches of opera tunes she recalled. When she was unsure of the words, she filled in the blanks with Italian-sounding phrases like "O, spaghettinio."

"I think I probably could have took him," said

Gunther, suddenly popping out of his reverie like someone's head surfacing from under water.

You never know, thought Betty as they rounded the bend for home, when someone heretofore perfectly reliable was going to go a little crazy. If I wasn't so stable, she thought, it would make me positively jumpy.

· Five ·

All week long Betty thought about ways she could make money for flowers. By Friday she had come up with only two solutions. She and Almira were sitting on the Grunts' porch, their pockets full of rock cookies.

"One," she said to Almira, as she crunched down on a cookie, "I could baby-sit. If I baby-sit every day until the Pork-Fry Festival, I might have enough money for flowers. But who is going to hire me to baby-sit? Two, I can find out where Garth is getting his money."

"The little sneak," put in Almira. She had four

younger brothers herself and had not a glorified opinion of the species.

"The little sneak, indeed," said Betty. "You know, I just can't imagine what Garth could be doing. I'm beginning to think that I smell an older brother."

"Yep," said Almira. "At six, their sneakiness is more in the form of grabbing the last biscuit and eating the evidence; but by the time they're fourteen, they've developed, well, something."

"Sophistication and subtlety," said Betty. "The important thing is that Janine Woodrow doesn't get to be the Pork-Fry Queen. Can you imagine?"

"Giving herself airs. Do you know, she actually told Delilah Diefenbacher that she hopes you get the money because it's so sad when poor folks are denied the few pleasures they got in this life?"

"I'll hate her till I die," exclaimed Betty. "And what does she mean 'poor folks'? Least my father's got a job."

Almira turned large liquid eyes on Betty, who swiftly bit down on her lip. Almira's father had been out of work for three months, and everyone knew the Poofpoffs were living on potatoes and lard.

"Oh, I didn't mean it that way, you know I didn't."

Almira started to cry. Then Betty started to cry, too. It seemed the least she could do.

"I don't know what we are going to do if Daddy doesn't find work soon," sobbed Almira.

"I just hate to be patronized. That rotten old Janine Woodrow," sobbed Betty.

Then below their high-pitched sobs, Betty sensed something wrong. She stopped sobbing and tried to figure out what in the world it was. She perked up her ears, and there it was: a sob unaccounted for. She looked around. She looked up, she looked down, and finally she saw Garth. He was hanging over the living-room windowsill and crying his eyes out.

"Garth Grunt," she ordered, "you get out here this minute. What do you mean sobbing like that?"

"I didn't know you wanted to be the Pork-Fry Queen," sobbed Garth. "I'll find some money for you. I know just where."

"Lard and potatoes," sobbed Almira.

"Oh, shut up," said Betty, wiping her eyes on the hem of her dress and getting down to business. "Where are we getting this money, Garth?"

"From Uncle Herman and Uncle Willy," said Garth.

Every summer the Grunt children spent a month on Uncle Herman and Uncle Willy's farm. Herman and Willy were Althea's uncles. They had lived forever sequestered with Aunt Hilda, who died before the children were born. She had cooked and cleaned and run all the errands in town. After

Aunt Hilda died, Uncle Willy made the infrequent trips to town, but he never looked at anyone and spoke only when absolutely necessary. It wasn't that he and Herman didn't like people; they were just shy. They were even afraid of the children. But Aunt Hilda had taken Althea and her brothers for summer visits ever since they were little. So naturally it followed that when Althea had children of her own they would carry on the tradition. Herman and Willy offered to take Treacle and Lolly's children, but Lolly said the devil was on the farm. Grant and Betty had spent an entire month looking for him but hadn't found him, so they guessed Lolly was mistaken.

Herman and Willy did their best to give the children a good month, letting them ride the donkey, Methuselah, saving Aunt Hilda's old fashion magazines to be cut up for paper dolls, playing their fiddles for them at night in the still country sunsets, letting them fish for surprises through a hole from the second-story bedroom down to the living room, where Uncle Willy and Uncle Herman waited to tie on toys they had been whittling all winter. One year they made the children a rocking horse, and when it wouldn't fit through the existing hole, Willy got his saw and made the hole bigger. They were wonderful uncles. You just couldn't talk to them. It made them blush. Betty loved them dearly and had no doubt they would give the children a fortune if they had one, but she thought of them in their old moth-eaten wool shirts and mud-encrusted trousers and said, "Willy and Herman haven't got any money, Garth. Are you trying to tell me they've been sending you nickels for baseball cards?"

"Forget the baseball cards," said Garth. "I'm talking about buried treasure."

"Huh," said Almira, who had stopped crying. "Buried treasure! Six-year-old brothers," she went on scathingly, "invent the most outrageous fibs. I am going on home now. I gotta get dinner for the boys. My mom is out looking for work again."

"I didn't mean to make you cry," said Betty, trying to be gracious and walk Almira to the bottom of the hill like a good best friend but secretly annoyed to pieces with her. Almira was always interrupting just when things were getting interesting. She was a dear girl but totally lacking in imagination. And, after all, her father would find work someday, and they'd get something to eat besides potatoes and lard eventually, and Althea was always taking over baked beans and stuff to help them along, and, good grief, she had just eaten about three dozen of their rock cookies, hadn't she? Jeez. Now, about that buried treasure, she thought, waving Almira off and running back. Just as she began to pump Garth, she heard boom boom boom, and up the hill thundered Lolly, a vision in a lemon-yellow housedress and dozens of little barrettes.

"Go get your mother," she hollered when she was in hollering distance.

Betty ran into the house and got Althea, who was scrubbing sheets. "Well, how do you do, Lolly," said Althea. "Haven't seen you in a dog's age."

"Myron and Percy been sick," said Lolly, panting. Lolly panted a good deal. She was of a body not made for hills. Betty had often heard her say that her dream was to live away someplace flat and arid, where the tumbleweed blew.

"I'm sorry to hear that," said Althea.

"Ague," said Lolly. To Lolly, everything—even Treacle's permanent heart condition—was ague. "I'm taking Treacle into town tomorrow. Reverend Emmanuel Horsefeathers is going to be speaking at the Seally Auditorium. He'll heal Treacle. I was going to have him heal the boys, but they woke up all better today. They couldn't've waited and have the Reverend do it properly, no, they had to up and heal themselves. They always was a couple of impatient little buggers. You know about the Reverend Emmanuel Horsefeathers, don't you?"

"I don't believe I do," said Althea, her forehead puckering. Betty knew that her mother hated the evangelist preachers whom Lolly was always trying to drag them to see. Betty didn't know much about them but was intrigued by their habit of rolling around and speaking in tongues.

"Those Holy Rollers," her mother would say in exasperation but refuse to elaborate on the subject. Betty had tried to find something about them in her school library, but it was somewhat limited on religious subjects.

"Well, anyhows, he's a most powerful preacher, I hear, and he has the gift. He has the gift," said Lolly.

"Has he?" said Althea noncommittally.

"I'm going to take your chillun with me. Now, don't you argue with me, Althea. Your own brother has suggested it. 'Take them poor little tykes next door that got no proper religion' is how he put it himself. And you know you can't deny your own brother, who is this very moment on his deathbed."

"His deathbed!" whispered Betty in disgust. Treacle never got any better, but he never got worse either.

"You *see*?" shrieked Lolly. "That child is whisperin'. Whisperin' in front of her elders. You better start bringing those children up, Althea, before the devil gets them. The devil sits around and waits for just such a golden opportunity."

"Don't you threaten me with the devil, Lolly Finnerty," said Althea. "And Betty, don't go whisperin'. You know better than that. If Treacle is really set on having my children go to listen, then I guess it's okay, but I won't have you taking them up to be healed. We have our own religious notions. Just because we don't go to *your* church doesn't mean we don't have a 'proper religion.' "

"Well, these preachers have done wonders for your own brother. Your own brother, Althea Finnerty Grunt. We are taking him in the back of the truck and we need your children to help carry him up to Jesus. Praise His name."

"Can I offer you a doughnut?" asked Althea, wishing to change the volatile subject of religion. And the grownups disappeared around the corner of the house.

"Well?" Betty said to Garth. "Buried treasure?"

Garth nodded. "You remember last summer when Methuselah kicked me in the shin?"

"Yes?" said Betty, climbing on the porch and sitting in a rocker. This was going to be a long story.

"Well, Uncle Herman felt real bad. I was bleeding and everything. You remember that?"

"It will live on in memory forever. Seared there, Garth, positively seared there with the great accidents of all time."

"It really made Uncle Herman feel bad."

"I think you said that."

"You keep mixing me up."

"I'm not mixing you up, I'm editing," said Betty.

"You sure are crabby," said Garth.

It was true, thought Betty, she felt amazingly crabby. She couldn't remember the last time she felt this crabby. It stuck in her craw that Janine Woodrow had made remarks about poor folks and she hadn't been there to answer back. She wanted to say something to Janine but was too embarrassed, and it made her want to punch out indiscriminately. She recognized this for the creepy behavior that it was, but *c'est la vie*, she thought.

"Okay," she said. "Just tell me the story."

"So he was bandaging my leg and I'm crying because it hurts like the dickens, and he's putting all this red junk on it and it's making it hurt worse. And then he says, 'You know, Aunt Hilda took all her money in the world and buried it someplace on the farm, and Willy and me don't know where because Aunt Hilda died and we ain't had time to look, bein' too busy with the cows and all, so maybe you'd like to have a look around.' "

"Wait a second," said Betty impatiently. "This is what Mac was talking about when he said Hilda's money, right? Why didn't you tell me he didn't mean money in Aunt Hilda's will or something, he meant this. This was the rumor no one bothered to do anything about. Well, did you look for it?" Imagine her little brother keeping a secret like this.

"Well, I did, but I couldn't find it, and I figured

it was an awful big farm and I sort of forgot about it."

"So," said Betty, getting up and pacing around the porch, avoiding rocking chairs and jamming rock cookies into her mouth one after the other in total exasperation. "So somewhere on Uncle Willy and Uncle Herman's farm there's money that no one is bothering to look for because they have forgotten about it or are TOO BUSY WITH THE COWS?"

"I guess that's about right," said Garth nervously.

"Meanwhile Ma is scrubbing her fingers to the bone, TO THE BONE, making an extra nickel here, an extra nickel there, so one of us can go to college someday. The one, I might add, who's got the brains to say, Let's not just let that money rot in the ground, let's DIG IT UP AND SPEND IT!"

"Well, I think we ought to give it to Uncle Willy and Uncle Herman," said Garth.

"If Uncle Herman and Uncle Willy wanted it, they would have looked for it. Oh," said Betty, stopping in her tracks as a dreadful thought occurred to her. "Now that Mac and Sam know Ma didn't get the money, do you think they are going to try to find it? They sounded pretty desperate."

"No," said Garth, putting on a serious expression as befits someone who has just been asked for his opinion. "I can't say that I do think that." This sounded very grown-up to him.

"You don't?" asked Betty, pouncing on him. "Why not?"

Garth hadn't realized that he would be asked for particulars, and he panicked. "Well, well, maybe I do think that!" he said. But he couldn't help but feel his opinion would not be required in the future.

"Oh honestly!" said Betty. "We just have to get there before them. Just support whatever I say from now on."

"Okay," said Garth. Finally, something he could manage.

At dinner that night, Althea mentioned to Grant that the next day he would be going with Betty and Garth to help Lolly carry Uncle Treacle to see an evangelical preacher in town. When Grant had stopped choking on his dinner, Althea said calmly, "Won't hurt you to get another point of view, even if you don't believe in it, which I trust you don't. I don't see Betty making such a ruckus."

Betty thought, She doesn't see Betty making a ruckus, because Betty likes to see the many facets of life. She regards every experience as a learning opportunity. It was this ardent curiosity that made one college material. Betty could just see herself chatting with the professors. She would wear stockings and pumps and her hair piled on her head. She would say, "Oh yes, I remember when my aunt"—pronounced "awnt," because by this time she would have a mid-Atlantic accent; she hadn't worked out the details of acquiring that yet—"forced me to go to an evangelical rally. Very amusing really!" And they would all laugh—no smile—in a superior sort of collegiate way.

Gunther stood up, took the napkin out of his collar, and burped. Grant and Garth looked at Betty, and she tried to smile at them in the superior collegiate way of her daydreams.

Grant said, "Oh, well, everyone knows she's just plain cracked."

Althea got up from the table and turned the radio on to a symphony, and Gunther went out to rock on the porch. Gretel came home.

"You won't believe what I saw down at the bus station," she said.

"Why, that's it. That's it," said Althea.

"What's it?" asked Gretel irritably, her story dangling from her tongue like a spider from a filament.

"The name of Betty's book. Betty, you must write a book and call it *Down at the Bus Station.* Why, think of all the material you have. Gretel brings you a story practically every night, that's all. We just have to get you some paper and pens."

"Well, Lord in heaven!" said Gretel. "I don't remember Betty saying she thought she could write a book, and anyway, I'm the one with the stories. Maybe I should write this here book you have in mind."

"Gretel Grunt, you know you got no inclination to write any such thing. Oh, isn't this music grand?" said Althea, sighing imperturbably.

"Well, anyhow. A man walks in with three hats on his head. You know, I ain't so surprised, because we see all kinds down at the bus station, and he wants to buy a one-way ticket to New York. So I give it to him, but I do kind of keep staring at his three hats. They're piled up on top of his head and, finally (he doesn't sound like a loon or anything), he looks at me and says, 'I see you staring at my three hats, sister. This is what's left of my business.' Turns out that he had a hat store for forty years. Forty years of successful hats salesmanship and then this depression come and take a chomp out of it, and all he's got left is three hats and practically no money, the creditors having took the rest. So with his last dime he's going to New York, where he has a brother also in the hat business, also broke."

"So why doesn't the brother come to Missouri?" says Garth.

"Oh . . . Garth," said Gretel, looking at him.

"Why would anyone want to come to Missouri?" asked Grant.

"I don't know," Gretel went on, "he didn't tell me any more. All I gets is a slice of life."

Gunther came in and stretched, then stood in the bosom of his family and barked, "Sunday drive. Sunday."

"Can we visit Willy and Herman?" asked Garth. Betty glared at him. He was supposed to follow *her* lead.

"Why, Garth," said Althea. "I like to see you children taking an interest in your kin."

"Hrunk," said Gunther.

"We could go Saturday night and come back Sunday before church," said Althea. "I'd have to stay up late Sunday to get the chores done, but that don't make no never mind. And, of course, it will frighten Herman and Willy to death to have to put us up like that."

"Could we, Pa?" asked Garth.

"Hrunk," said Gunther, and, turning the radio to the news, was soon fast asleep.

· Six ·

Early the next morning, the children's mother shooed them out the door and over to Lolly's. Myron and Percy were already in the backyard, scrubbed and dressed in their best. They were nine and ten, but with their creepy composure they could have been middle-aged businessmen.

"Howdya do, cousins?" they asked in their mushy little voices. They made Betty's skin crawl. She didn't think her own family was any too bright; but there was something so repulsive about her cousins' squeaky-clean goodness—combined with their not very brightness—that made Betty want to wash herself all over whenever she was forced to have contact with them.

"Your Uncle Treacle is jest inside having a shave," said Myron. He pulled Grant aside, leaned over, and whispered something in his ear. Percy joined them for a short huddle, and Betty saw Myron and Percy hand Grant something. A small religious tract, perhaps? She was about to ask, when they suddenly disbanded and Percy said, "Mama's shaving him."

"Then we can carry him to the truck."

"Carry him to be healed."

"Carry him to Jesus."

"Hallelujah."

"Oh, shut up," said Grant.

"Chillun! Chillun!" called Lolly. Betty hated her aunt saying "chillun." It was ten thousand times worse than "yeller," which was bad enough.

"Chillun, your daddy is ready to be carried out."

The five children went in and lifted Uncle Treacle's cot up and carried it outside under the helpful direction of Lolly, who yelled "LORD OF MERCY!" every time they dropped him, which was frequently. Finally, the truck was on the road, with the children and a sleeping Treacle in the back and Lolly in the front singing hymns in a high, squeaky voice.

Myron and Percy weren't much for conversation, being immersed in prayer in preparation for their encounter with the Reverend Emmanuel Horse-feathers. Betty, Grant, and Garth were too disgusted to say much themselves, besides feeling that they were in the enemy camp and anything they said would be used against them.

The Seally Auditorium parking lot was full. People were standing in crowds waiting to get in. Betty felt embarrassed to be carrying a man on a bed, even if it was her own Uncle Treacle, but as she got closer she saw a lot of beds being carried, and began to feel less conspicuous. Lolly just kept elbowing people aside with her huge dimpled arms and saying, "Praise the Lord, praise the Lord, praise His name, getoutomyway, praise the Lord, hallelujah." Finally, they had gotten as far as Lolly's elbows would take them, and they were forced to wait in line.

It was a warm spring day and the wait was a long one. Betty shifted from one foot to the other. Grant and Garth, who realized they were going nowhere quickly, gave up and sat on the curb. Myron and Percy seemed oblivious to the heat and had their eyes closed in prayer—or perhaps, thought Betty, it's their way of shutting Lolly out. Lolly stood on her two monstrous feet, with her mouth pursed and angry and her face reddened with the heat, looking stonily across the street. Betty wished she could sit down, too, but a girl couldn't sit on the curb in her best going-to-church dress, so she continued to shift uncomfortably.

Across the street was a shoe store, a news stall, some apple stands, and a candy store with a soda fountain. Betty looked longingly at the candy displayed in the window, and then her eyes went in to the fountain with its gleaming counter and stools. A couple was sitting there, evidently having sodas. She wondered what it must be like to be able to walk into a candy store and have a soda. As she was wondering, the couple rose to leave, and who should the woman be but Gretel. It couldn't be Gretel! Gretel was working, and besides, Gretel didn't have a boyfriend. This man was tall and handsome, and he had his hand around Gretel's waist as he paid for the sodas. Betty's mouth fell open and she made an involuntary "gak" sound. This caused Lolly to look at her swiftly and suspiciously. Lolly's eyes followed Betty's, and she went "gak" as well.

"Well, my Lord in heaven, my Lord in heaven," said Lolly. "Betty Grunt, is that your sister, Gretel, or do my eyes deceive me?"

"I dunno," said Betty, but Gretel and the man were walking out and there was no mistaking that it was Gretel.

"Isn't your sister supposed to be working now? Even as we stand here? Betty Grunt, I'll speak to your mama about this. I will speak to her first thing. I always said to Treacle, 'Treacle, those chillun are going to go bad in that house. They're going to go *bad*.' Pray for her, Betty, and pray you don't turn out the same."

Betty looked at Lolly muttering to herself, and she wished she were at home. She wished she could run down the street and warn Gretel. She didn't care if Gretel had ditched work. If she had a chance to have a soda at a real soda fountain, she would grab it, too. And if Gretel did this regularly, if Gretel had a secret life, well, then, Lolly was going to spoil it for her sure as shooting. Betty worried about it all during the service. She worried about it so much that, even when she helped carry Uncle Treacle up and right during the blessing Lolly had sneezed violently over a surprised Reverend Horsefeathers—who proceeded to take out a rather large handkerchief and wipe himself with a kind of fastidious care somehow not in keeping with one empowered to banish earthly germs—she could take no pleasure in it at all. "Are you healed, brother?" shouted the Reverend Horsefeathers when every last droplet had been wiped away. "I am," said Uncle Treacle. But, thought Betty, what else could a polite person say?

They carried Uncle Treacle back to the truck finally and sped home. Lolly seemed satisfied. At home she was in such a frenzy of feeling that she appeared to have forgotten about Gretel. She had a glazed look in her eye and kept muttering about how Jesus lives and walking into walls. The children put Uncle Treacle in his bedroom and escaped.

On their way back from Lolly's house, Betty explained to Grant and Garth what she and Lolly had seen.

"Whew," whistled Grant.

"What's a double life?" asked Garth.

"It means she's doing things we don't get wind of," said Grant.

"We don't know anything really," said Betty. "All we know is that she said she would be working Saturday. Well, she didn't say it exactly, but we assumed it because she always works Saturday."

"Who cares if she does snitch on Gretel?" said Grant.

"I do," said Betty, "because Lolly is going to come clumping up the hill and make a big stink about it, and it just makes me mad clean through. So, do you want to hear about my plan or not?"

"I dunno," said Grant.

Betty took hold of his shirtfront and breathed hotly up into his face. *"Blood,"* she enunciated crisply, *"is thicker than water."*

"Let go," said Grant, pulling away. But Betty

could tell he was weakening, so she sat him and Garth down and explained over and over her little plan of counterattack, until they got it straight.

They waited for Gretel to get home and, since Althea wanted to get some of the Sunday chores out of the way, sat down to a late, twilight supper. Gretel said nothing during the meal about a young man, even though Grant dropped a hint every other bite along the lines of "Good sodas down at the ole candy store" and "A girl ought to have a young man" and subtle things of this nature.

After supper, scrubbed and begloved, the Grunts climbed into the yellow car. As Althea set her hat straight and Gunther pulled at his trouser legs and Gretel whined about missing her Saturday night out, the family heard boom boom boom up the hill.

"Dad blast it, what do that woman want now?" said Gunther and started the engine but stopped it when Althea said, "Oh wait, Gunther, it's my own sister-in-law, for pity's sake." She called down the hill, where they saw Lolly's face appearing over the crest like a malevolent moon. "Hello there, Lolly!"

"I got . . . WHOA," bellowed Lolly like a bassoon. "I got something to . . . (pant pant pant) . . . say. And say . . . (pant, pant, pant) . . . it I will."

"Hit it," said Betty, and she and Grant and Garth began a rousing chorus of "When the Saints Go Marching In."

"Oh when the saints," began Betty.

"I said the saints," droned Grant.

"Go marching in," sang Betty.

"Go marching in, sing it, sister," crooned Garth.

"Oh when the saints go marching in," they sang together.

"Listen up," hollered Lolly.

"Louder," whispered Betty. They began to sing for all their worth, and Gretel, usually aloof, joined in. It was such a pleasure to drown out Lolly. To hoist her on her own musical petard, as it were.

"Oh Lord, I want, I want, I want, I want, to be in those numbers, oh hallelujah," sang Gretel. "Oh when the saints go marching in."

"Just going on our little drive," yelled Althea, all smiles and waves.

Gunther started the car again.

"Well, wait up there," said Lolly, but was drowned out.

Gunther put the car into the wrong gear and drove backward up the hill, ramming into the side of the porch.

"What's that dern porch doing there?" he growled, and tried to drive forward. But Lolly waddled up behind them and lay hold of the bumper.

"Now listen, Althea, I come up here for a reason."

"When the sun, dodododo, begin to shine, dodododo," sang the children.

"Hallelujah!" said Lolly, unable to stop herself. "Now, Althea Finnerty Grunt, you listen to me."

But either Althea was tired of listening to Lolly or she didn't hear her over the children's singing, for she got out of the car, adjusted her skirt, and gave the car a firm push. This caused Lolly to teeter and fall backward, but with the car starting suddenly forward, Althea had to run ahead, leap onto the running board, and climb in. Apparently under the impression that Lolly had also been trying to push the car forward, she smiled and called, "Thanks for your help! My," she said, patting her hair back into place, "that singing sounds real nice in the car, doesn't it? It sort of echoes. All you children have such lovely voices!"

Gunther hadn't driven the car for a whole week, and, thought Betty, it was like starting from square one. They flew down the hill, their hearts in their mouths, and it wasn't until they were on the road that Althea remembered Lolly. "Oh, my gosh, I wonder what Lolly wanted. Do you think we ought to go back?" she asked, trying to turn and peer up the hill at Lolly, who was making her awkward way to a standing position.

"NO!" shouted the children all at once.

"Hrunk," said Gunther.

"I suppose whatever it was will keep till we get back," said Althea uncertainly. "Why don't you children sing us another song?"

"I'm no choirboy," said Grant. So they drove on in silence until Betty caught his eye, and then even he couldn't help snorting with laughter when he thought about how they had scuttled Lolly.

By the time the Grunts pulled into the road leading to Willy and Herman's farm, it was dark. "Just look at them stars," said Althea. She still disapproved of the car, but it did take her to see her family and she couldn't help but be happy about that.

Willy and Herman, hearing the car bumping its way up their road, came out to the porch and stared at them in the starlight.

Althea stepped out and hugged them, much to their embarrassment. "How good to see you, Willy and Herman. We come for a little visit. I hope we're not intruding," she went on, dragging her sleepy family up the porch steps.

"Hrunk," said Gunther.

Willy and Herman shook their heads but continued to stare in awe at the big yellow car.

Finally, Herman gestured toward it.

"Oh, it's ours!" said Althea, laughing. "At least for the moment. A little old lady, who had no more use for it, sold it to Gunther. But, of course, we can't keep it. Not forever."

Betty noticed that her mother left out the part about her defunct college-education fund.

Herman came down from the porch and stroked the side of the car with his big gnarled farmer's hand, then he gestured to the house. "I'll get some beds made up."

"I'll get the blankets," said Willy, evidently thankful for an opportunity to disappear.

Betty and Gretel climbed up to the attic room. It was where they slept every summer, and Betty loved it. Two huge ancient trees rose up in front of the window, and when she looked at them at night through the tattered chiffon curtains, she felt safe. All was right with the world while these two giants stood serenely guarding her and her family. She was about to doze off, when Gretel, who slept next to her, pinched her wrist.

"Ow!" yelled Betty.

"Hush, I was just seeing if you were awake. You and Lolly saw me at the candy store with Clarence, didn't you?"

"How'd you know?" asked Betty.

"I saw you, too. I didn't know you had seen me, but when I got up to go to the ladies', I saw all of you across the street holding Uncle Treacle in that bed. I was never so embarrassed in my life. I kept thinking, What if they call out when Clarence and I go out? He doesn't have a, well, a real accurate picture of our family."

"You mean you told him a bunch of lies about us?"

"I sure did. I guess Lolly wants to tell Ma she saw me with a man when I was supposed to be working, but it weren't such a big deal. I got Harriet covering for me on Saturday mornings so I can get a soda or something with Clarence. He's a college boy. I met him at the bus station when he was buying a ticket. The first time he took me out for a soda, I thought, I dunno, he must be pretty lonely to take out just anyone, even me, but then he asked me a second time. I mean, you'd think a good-looking guy like that would have the pick of the coeds. I don't care if Ma knows about it or not. I'm much more scared that he'll find out about our family. Clarence is rich. He's studying biology and stuff. Anyhow, I appreciate what you and the boys did for me, but it won't stop Lolly from telling. She'll just keep coming back, and you can't drown her out forever. I just thought I'd let you know why I was being so sneaky, not mentioning Clarence and stuff."

"You mean you're not being sneaky because you're ashamed of Clarence?"

"Lord, no," said Gretel.

"Only because you're ashamed of us?"

"That's it. I'm glad you understand," said Gretel, sighing, and she rolled over contentedly to go to sleep.

What in the world was a college boy doing with Gretel? And poor Gretel, thought Betty. To think of her sister's ignominious fate when Clarence discovers his test rats are smarter than his date. She looked out at the big trees and sighed.

· Seven ·

The next morning, Willy and Herman were out in the fields by the time Garth and Betty got up, but they had left a huge country breakfast on the stove. Gretel and Grant were still sleeping, Gunther had gone out to help Willy and Herman, and Althea was enjoying a moment of leisure, rocking on the porch before cooking the Sunday dinner.

"Come on," said Garth to Betty, and they went down the pasture to sit on the fence and survey the acres of rolling hills. "Where do we look?"

"Well," said Betty, thinking things through, "for one thing, she wouldn't just bury it in the pasture, or she'd never find it either. It has to be someplace where she could get her hands on it quickly and where it wouldn't be apt to be dug up by someone plowing a field or by animals. It's got to be someplace well marked or conspicuous in some manner."

They both surveyed the farm—from the big barn to the creaky house and outbuildings.

"Suppose she put it in the outhouse?" said Garth, giggling. "Who's gonna be brave enough to fetch it?"

"I'd do it if it meant I could be the Pork-Fry Queen," said Betty. "Here comes Grant down the hill. Are we going to tell him?"

"I dunno," said Garth. "Means splitting it three ways."

"What are you going to do with yours, anyway?" asked Betty, suddenly interested. "You can't possibly spend it all on baseball cards."

"No," said Garth, and picked a long piece of grass and chewed on the root. "I wanna be a baseball player. I guess I'd just save mine, and then, when it was time, use it to go off to the training camps and show them my stuff."

"I didn't know you wanted to be a baseball player," said Betty.

"Sure. I guess anyone would," said Garth.

"Not Grant," said Betty as they watched him come down the hill, parting the long grass with his swagger. "I think his aim is to join the criminal element."

Grant hitched himself up on the fence post and looked at them truculently. "What are you guys off by yourselves for?" he asked.

Garth turned to Betty. She figured that if they found the money, there would be less for all of them, and what had Grant ever done for her. On the other hand, the chances of their finding it with one more person searching were better. Come to think of it, even though Grant wouldn't lend her any money to be Pork-Fry Queen, he did save her life from, as it turned out, her own kith and kin. She told him about Hilda's stash.

"Nyah," said Grant when she was done. "It's a crazy story. What makes them think Hilda even had any money?"

"Well, I guess her own brothers would know if she had any money."

"Then why hasn't anyone been turning this place upside down for it?"

"Because," said Betty, sighing resignedly, "they were BUSY WITH THE COWS."

"You're gonna spend the whole morning digging up pasture for a crummy dollar to become a crummy Pork-Fry Queen?"

"You've got an easier way to make a dollar, I suppose?" said Betty.

"I make more than that in an afternoon pitching pennies," said Grant.

"Oh, Grant, you don't pitch pennies, do you?" wailed Betty.

"Why not? I'm not gonna graduate school anyhow, and it don't matter if I do. You know well as I do, I'm gonna go work for the railroad just like Pa. That is, if I'm lucky. I won't ever have enough money to have my own farm or nothing. That's what I'd like. Not that *you* care."

"Well, I can't picture you as a farmer anyhow," said Betty.

"We can't all be la-di-da artists and writers."

"I just can't see you doing anything that involves real"—and here, Betty fell right off the fence, dissolved in hysterical laughter brought on by what was beginning to seem like insurmountable odds against becoming the Pork-Fry Queen—"work." She rolled over and over, until she rolled into an unfortunate reminder that the pasture was really for the cows.

"Oh criminy!" she yelled.

Garth covered his mouth with his hands and gasped.

Grant burst into laughter now, but was careful to hang on to the fence.

"Oh, stop laughing. I haven't got any other clothes here. What am I going to do?"

"It's your own fault," said Grant. "You think you're so smart."

"Ma's gonna kill me. I can't go to dinner like this."

"There's the dress-up clothes," said Garth.

There was a trunk of Hilda's old clothes in the attic, and until Gretel and Betty had grown too old for them they had whiled away many a summer afternoon playing dress-up.

"Well, I'm gonna look pretty silly in one of Hilda's old dresses, but I guess it's better than this," said Betty, sniffing in disgust.

"You know," said Grant, "if Hilda hid the money anywhere, it's probably someplace kind of obvious. She was just a little brighter than the cows, wasn't she? Isn't that what Ma used to say about her?"

"That's what Ma said, but maybe . . ." Betty began, when she put her foot in a hole and fell on her face again.

"Jeez, you're clumsy," said Garth sympathetically.

Betty brushed herself off, then stopped. She jumped out of the hole and began racing around the pasture. "Look," she yelled, "another one. And another one!"

"Another what?" asked Grant.

"Hole!" yelled Betty, but she was off down the pasture to where Uncle Willy was working.

"Have Sam and Mac been here?" she asked, racing up to him. "Have they?"

"Yep," said Uncle Willy, not glancing up.

"Well, what did they say they wanted?" she demanded.

"Wanted to dig holes in the pasture," said Willy.

"Why?" asked Betty.

"Dunno," said Willy.

"Did they find anything?" asked Betty.

"Nope," said Uncle Willy. "Told them to stop. Derned foolishness, and the cows were tripping. Said they had their own farm now, so I told them to go dig holes in their own pasture. Never did like that pair."

"Did they go away?"

"Yep."

"Have they come back since?"

"Nope."

"Thanks," said Betty, and raced to tell the boys. When she explained to them that Sam and Mac were on the trail, Grant grew grave. Somehow, having grownups believing in the money made it more real to him. He thought it over as they went into the house and climbed upstairs.

"So, they either found something, have given up the idea of there being any money, or are still planning on coming back to look," he said, pacing up and down in the attic, where Betty was searching for something to wear in the dress-up trunk. Hilda had been only five feet tall, so fortunately the dresses were not too long for Betty but Hilda had been, near as Betty could judge, a right porker, and the dresses were more like short tents. This was fine when Betty was playing dress-up, but not so good when she was hoping her mother wouldn't notice that she wasn't wearing her own dress. She chose a brown-checked gingham and an old bathrobe cord that was in the trunk to belt it around her waist. Then she went behind some boxes to change.

"Children! Dinner!" called their mother. The children groaned. Here on the farm, Herman and Willy had been at work for hours and would be ready for a big dinner, but the children had eaten breakfast only a short while ago. Grant, Betty, and Garth washed and went down. After grace had been said and everyone had loaded their plates with roast chicken and dumplings, Althea said, "What in the world are you wearing, Betty?"

"It's one of Hilda's old dresses. We used to wear them for dressing up."

"Well, you can run right upstairs and take it off," said Althea. "Imagine, coming down to Sunday dinner in dress-up clothes. I thought I raised you righter than that."

"Can't," said Betty. "My dress got dirty and I had to change into something."

"Well, whatever happened?" asked Althea.

"You don't want to know at dinner," said Betty. Garth and Grant snickered.

"Oh, for heaven's sake. What a mess," said Althea, guessing in a trice. "After we wash up these dishes, we are going to head on back home, so I won't have time to wash your dress. You'll just have to wear it, dirty or not."

"Ooo," said Grant, holding his nose. "I ain't riding home with her and that smelly ole dress."

"Can we please not talk about this at dinner?" asked a long-suffering Gretel.

"Pooh," said Garth, holding *his* nose.

"Oh . . . Garth," said their mother absently.

"She can have Hilda's old dress, Althea," said Willy, putting his chin down into his chest and generally trying to turn himself inside out with embarrassment. "We only kept them dresses for the girls to play in. They is all Hilda left."

" 'Cept her diary," put in Herman, turning his red face away from the table and addressing the buffet so as not to have to look at anyone while speaking.

"That's very kind of you, Willy, Herman. That's what we'll do then."

The children cleared the table. It was while they were all tucking into their rhubarb pie that Betty had the idea. It was so startling that she dropped her fork and stared right at her uncles, who went crimson and put their hands in front of their faces on the pretext of scratching their foreheads. She was so sure that the idea must have occurred to Grant or Garth that she kicked them both simultaneously under the table.

"Ow," they squawked and kicked her back.

She kicked them again. They kicked her. She kicked back, and Garth's chair fell over.

"WHAT IN BLAZES IS THE MATTER WITH YOU CHILDREN?" hollered Gunther, his eyebrows coming together and making a long furry snake instead of two cute little caterpillars.

"*She* started it," said Grant.

"Go do the dishes!" roared their father.

Betty slunk off to the kitchen, so furious that she contemplated not even telling the boys about her idea. The men, having eaten, went out to have a better look at the yellow car, while Gretel, Althea, and Betty did the dishes. When the kitchen was all cleaned, Betty found Grant and Garth tossing stones in the backyard and came up and hit them on the head.

"Hey!" said Grant, and put up his fists.

"You thickheaded, cow-brained, no-account poop," she said. "Didn't anything at dinner catch your interest?"

"Well, I did develop a taste for that rhubarb pie."

"Nobody makes a rhubarb pie like Ma," said Garth, repeating a familial refrain.

"Nobody," echoed Grant.

"I see in the future I will have to use the two of

you purely as manual laborers," said Betty in disgust.

"If you're gonna stand there and talk in puzzles, why don't you just get lost?"

"Yeah, good riddance," said Garth.

"*Think!*" shouted Betty. "Okay, here's a clue. Hilda and her money. Money to be the Pork-Fry Queen. Money to buy farmland. Money to become a major baseball pitcher."

"Catcher," said Garth.

"Catcher?" said Betty.

"Catcher?" said Grant. "Who wants to be a catcher?"

"I do," said Garth.

"Anyhow," said Grant, "I don't believe there is any money."

"Well," said Betty, getting really angry and stamping around in circles. "If you don't believe in anything, Grant, if you're so stupid and pigheaded you don't believe in anything, then good luck to you. You won't ever be anything. You'll never be a farmer, you'll never be a railroad worker. Nothing is anything without the idea first. I'll tell you what I think, I don't think either of you is stupid. I think you're both just too lazy to kick your brains into gear."

Grant and Garth scuffed their toes in the dirt and spat a few times, which, they had learned from the menfolk, was the thing to do when you couldn't think of what to say.

"What kind of idea do you want us to have?" asked Grant sullenly.

"I want," hissed Betty, "for you to *think* what might have been said at dinner about Hilda that might have some bearing on our finding *the money.*"

"Well, jeez, if you know, how come we have to think?" whined Garth.

"Because," Betty continued to hiss, "we are all in this together now, and I am not doing your *work for you*. And because," she continued in a very scary snakelike manner that caused both Garth and Grant to back up several feet, "I . . . am . . . try-ing . . . to . . . help . . . you . . . discipline . . . your . . . lumplike . . . underused . . . brains . . . and . . . mold . . . you . . . into . . . the . . . fine . . . creatures . . . I'M SURE YOU WERE MEANT TO BE!"

"Oh," said Garth.

"THE DIARY!" shouted Grant, and looked very pleased with himself. No one had ever hinted that he might not be as dumb as he looked.

"That's right," said Betty, suddenly exhausted, "the diary."

"You mean," said Garth, "she might have put something in the diary about where she hid the money?"

"Of course she did. What else would she have to put in there? Nothing special could really have happened on the farm. Why, that money was probably the biggest event of her whole existence here. We just have to ask Uncle Herman for the diary, and you know him, he'd do anything for us."

After Althea had called the children to the car and they had put on their white gloves and said goodbye, Garth, the elected spokesperson, took Herman aside and whispered to him that he'd like to see Hilda's diary. Herman turned red and whispered something back. It wasn't until the car was rolling along that Garth murmured to Grant and Betty, "The diary's in the library!"

· Eight ·

"Oh, good heavens!" wailed Betty, directing an accusing finger at Garth.

"What? What? What?" asked Garth, cowering in the apple tree.

Due to the secrecy of their mission, they had not heard the details of Herman and Garth's conversation until the next day after school, when they met in one of the apple trees in the orchard.

"Why didn't you ask him for the diary if he knew where it was? It's no good for us to *know* where it is. We have to read it."

"Well, heck," said Garth. "What good is it to read

it and know where the money is if we can't dig for it anyhow?"

"He's got you there," said Grant, and snorted.

Betty closed her eyes and hung by her knees. She hoped all the blood running to her brain would give her an idea.

"Besides, what's the rush?" asked Grant. "Why don't we wait until August when we are there all month and got nothing better to do anyhow?"

"That's fine for you and Garth. Your baseball playing and farming aren't going anywhere, but I need the money to be the Pork-Fry Queen."

"I'll be glad to lend you some money at a special rate of interest," said Grant, plucking leaves off the trees and looking shifty-eyed. "That is, now that I know you may come into some money and have some way to actually pay me off, which I didn't reckon you had before."

"How do you get your money anyhow, Grant?" asked Betty.

"Wouldn't you like to know? Let's just say I have my ways."

"Well, I think that's downright selfish," said Betty. "Just you think of Ma and Pa slaving away day after day to keep food on the table while you're off pitching pennies. That *is* where you said you get it, isn't it?"

"He's not selfish," said Garth. "He buys me base-ball cards."

"You shut up," said Grant furiously.

"I said you weren't selfish, is all," said Garth.

"So that's where you get all those baseball cards. Well, Garth Grunt, you'll be sorry to know those baseball cards were acquired with ill-gotten gains, and I wouldn't have that on my conscience," said Betty, swinging out of the tree.

"Like heck they were," said Grant. "I earned that money fair and square."

"How?" asked Betty.

"Wouldn't you like to know?" said Grant with tedious repetitiveness. "Besides, you're just a crazy girl wanting to dress up and be ham queen."

"Pork-Fry Queen."

"Sooey, sooey," called Grant, as Betty walked with dignity back to the house. "Sooey, sooey, sooey."

The next day at school, Miss Fenster called Betty in at recess.

"Yes, Miss Fenster?" asked Betty, eyeing her neck but trying to look as if she wasn't. Miss Fenster's neck had little rolls of skin that sat one on top of the other like a stacking toy; it was the unfortunate way people in Miss Fenster's family responded to the demands of gravity and aging and Betty realized her teacher couldn't help it, but she did wonder why Miss Fenster never noticed that the talcum powder, which she apparently put on with a trowel, tended to pile up and cake in the skin folds, so that her neck had the odd appearance of being cemented together, skin ring by skin ring. It was nearly impossible not to stare at it.

"Betty Grunt, I don't believe I have received your dollar for flowers yet, or am I mistaken?"

"No, Miss Fenster, you haven't," said Betty.

"I thought not. So I have decided, in order to save you embarrassment, I would ask Janine Woodrow to be Pork-Fry Queen. We won't mention it again. Least said, soonest mended."

"I'm going to get the money, Miss Fenster. I have two more weeks until I have to have it in, don't I? You said the last day in May."

"Is that what I said?"

"Yes, ma'am."

"Just where do you plan to get this dollar, Betty?"

"From . . . an uncle," said Betty.

"Humph," said Miss Fenster, implying in that syllable what she thought the chances were of Betty having an uncle who wasn't curled up in the gutter with a bottle of Old Crow.

"So, if you don't mind," said Betty, "I'd like to wait until then."

"I hope I don't detect an imperilous attitude, Betty Grunt. I don't suppose you even know what 'imperilous' means, do you?"

"No, I don't," said Betty.

"It means bossy, Betty," said Miss Fenster, pursing her lips.

"Sort of like imperious," said Betty.

"Don't get smart with me, miss. The word is *imperilous.*"

"Yes, ma'am."

"You may go to recess now, Betty. I'll wait until the last day of May, but not a second, not a second longer."

Almira waved to her from the grass outside. The children had two recess options. Either they could push each other around and try to avoid having their shins kicked and their noses bloodied, or they could sit on the grass and watch the children on the concrete pushing one another around and engaging in the aforementioned exercise. Almira and Betty were pacifists.

"What did Miss Fenster the Dumpster want?" asked Almira.

"She wanted me to say it was okay for Janine to be the Pork-Fry Queen, but I wouldn't. I've got to get that dollar. I won't ever be voted to anything like this again. I very much fear, Almira, that I am just going to get more thick-waisted and frizzy-haired as I get older."

"What makes you think that?"

"Look around at young girls and middle-aged women, and draw your own conclusions. Girls start out sleek with long, straight, shiny hair and end up in their middle years with thick waists and short, curly hair. So if you start *out* with a thick waist and frizzy hair, you are *doomed*. If I am *ever* going to be glamorous, this may be my last chance and I had better grab it."

Almira nodded. She was a good friend, of the type who makes no attempt to dissuade one from one's own blacker thoughts.

"Well, anyhow, you're awful smart," said Almira. "My mother says that the way you talk, you should go into politics."

"Big consolation," said Betty, dropping her head into her hands. *"She,"* Betty went on, nodding toward Janine Woodrow, who sat sedately on the grass in slim, blond-headed splendor, "will always be chosen to be the queen of things. I just sneaked through. It was a fluke that will never more repeat itself, and that ole Fenster the Dumpster can't even let miracles be miracles."

"Yeah, and I know why. Mr. Woodrow always gives Janine's teachers a twenty percent discount at Woodrow's department store. Miss Fenster is probably bucking for fifty percent. And Janine goes around telling everyone how sweet you are, how you deserve to be the Pork-Fry Queen, how terrible it is that your family is so very, very poor that they can't even afford flowers for the Pork Fry. How humiliated she would be if her family ever fell on such hard times. How . . ."

"All right, all right, I get the picture," said Betty, who couldn't help but feel that Almira was dragging this on longer than necessary. "If I had no conscience at all and were the scum of the earth and didn't worry about Christian virtues, I would take the dollar from my brother, Grant, even if it is ill-gotten gains."

"Where does *he* get it?" asked Almira.

"He says," Betty paused dramatically, "he . . . pitches . . . pennies."

"Ooooo," said Almira. A stunned silence followed.

"Nah," said Almira finally. "Listen, you know where they pitch pennies? A bunch of tough old out-of-work guys down by the hardware store, and I pass there every day. I never once saw Grant there, or any kid for that matter. You got to have pennies to begin with. I think Grant's full of hot air."

"Well, he has to make the money somewhere. He says it's in an honest fashion, but why should I believe him? If it's so honest, why doesn't he tell us about it?"

"Because he wants to act tough. I'll tell you what," said Almira, "why don't we spy on him?"

"We can't follow him around all day. He'd be sure to see us," said Betty. "And besides, I got to find a way to make some money."

"Well, maybe we can find out what he's doing, and if it's so honest, you can do it, too."

"I suppose it's worth a try," said Betty. "Why

don't you come to my house Saturday morning and wait behind the car for me? I'll hide there, too, and when he comes out we'll follow him."

"Okeydokey," said Almira.

Saturday morning it rained, but when Betty crept behind the car, she found a dripping and sneezing Almira loyally crouched there.

"Now, all we got to do is wait," said Betty.

Time ticked on. Grant was slow getting up and breakfasting. Finally, as they saw him jump down the porch steps, the sun appeared. He had just hit the ground when Althea came out and called, "Grant! Grant!"

Grant looked as if he was about to pretend not to hear and to take a powder, but evidently his better side prevailed and he stopped and turned around. "What, Ma?"

"Can you fix those porch slats for me? I been meaning to fix them, but I ain't got time with all the laundry and such."

"You mean right now, Ma?"

"You aren't going anyplace important, are you?"

"No, but listen, I just got to run over and tell someone something, and then I'll be right back."

"Grant, I really want those porch slats fixed. It looks so awful with them dented in that way."

"I promise, Ma. I won't be gone more than ten minutes or so."

"All right, then," said Althea, and went inside.

They saw Grant race down the hill.

"Hurry! Hurry!" said Almira, nudging Betty. But Betty was on her feet and running before Almira could say more.

Betty raced to the cover of the trees that were between their hill and Aunt Lolly's and she and Almira ran through the forest to the bottom of the hill. It was slower than going straight down the meadow, but they remained hidden. At the bottom, they saw three pairs of legs under some bushes, and Betty grabbed Almira's arm, gesturing her to stop.

"Those are Grant's feet," she whispered. She put her finger to her lips, and the two of them tiptoed to the bushes.

"So, boys," said Grant. "What'll it be this week? Your nickels are at the ready, I trust?"

"Me and Percy been talking it over," came cousin Myron's voice. "And we think a fifty-fifty split is too much. I mean, it's our collection money, after all."

"It's your collection money, but I'm the one who can get into town for the goodies. If you boys think ole Lolly will let you go to the drugstore and spend your Sunday-school money on penny candy, why, you be my guests," said Grant.

Betty could hear a heavy sigh.

"You're heading for the devil with that kind of outlook, Brother Grant."

"Why did he call him brother?" whispered Almira.

"Oh, it's that phony-baloney brotherhood stuff, now shhh," said Betty, hoping Almira hadn't blown their cover.

"Yeah, yeah, yeah," said Grant. "Fork over the nickels."

"Well, brother, you'd think after two years you'd give us a discount," said Myron. "We being such good customers and all."

"Listen, you greedy little pig," said Grant. "All you do is stuff your faces with penny candy all week. I don't even spend my cut. You want to talk about higher purposes . . . Oh, never mind."

"We're going to pray for you, Brother Grant," said Percy in his mushy-mush voice.

"You do that," said Grant. "Now, let's see the color of your money."

"Doesn't he know what color it is?" whispered Almira.

"Of course he knows what color it is. Now shhh," whispered Betty so violently that Almira fell off her haunches backward and made a crunching noise. Betty grabbed her. She had heard enough anyway. She dragged Almira away and pulled her under a pine tree to piece things together.

"Aunt Lolly is a monster, and she never lets those two out of their own yard. I guess all the money they get is for the collection plate, and she gives it to them early or else they just save it until the following Saturday. Anyhow, Grant must take it to the drugstore and spend it on penny candy for them. He gets half and they get half and he buys some baseball cards for Garth."

"Well, I suppose it's an honest enterprise," said Almira doubtfully.

"Of course, Lolly *does* give it to them to put in the collection plate," said Betty.

"Still, can charity ever be forced?" asked Almira.

"I believe it can," said Betty ruminatively. "But that is neither here nor there. And besides, Lolly beats those two with a stick from time to time, and Ma says she thinks that Lolly has knocked the sense right out of them."

"Not a very nice family," said Almira primly.

"No, not a nice family at all," said Betty. She and Almira just loved to discuss things like this. "Of course, my mama says that, with Treacle being in bed and Lolly having to nurse him, tend their vegetable patch, take care of the children, and do all the housekeeping, she is under tremendous pressure."

"That's never an excuse, I don't think, do you?" asked Almira.

"Never," said Betty.

So deep were they in this philosophical discussion, they didn't hear footsteps behind them until suddenly a shadow towered over them, and, looking up, they saw the menacing, large-toothed, mammoth outline of Lolly, ready to pounce.

· Nine ·

Almira screamed. Betty was too terrified to scream. Lolly reached down and grabbed the girls by their collars and pulled them to their feet.

"Help! Help!" called Betty.

"I heard you!" roared Lolly in their ears. "I was weeding vegetables just three feet away. I heard every miserable word." And here she shook the girls until their bones rattled.

"Oh, my heavens," whispered Almira.

"Put us down," said Betty. "We didn't do anything. It's your own sons."

"Myron and Percy would never do sech things,

you miserable, sinful, spiteful bit of goods," said Lolly, dragging Betty and Almira up the hill.

"Ow, you're *choking* me," yelled Betty.

"Serves you right. It's not me choking you, it's your own lying words, praise the Lord, praise the Lord," said Lolly, not even looking back at the girls as she dragged them along. They couldn't tell whether Lolly meant to haul them to her own lair or return them to the Grunts' house, where Betty felt fairly sure Althea would rescue them. At first, as Lolly seemed to veer right, Betty held out hope for her own house; but then Lolly turned abruptly, took them on the path, underneath her laundry lines, through her vegetable patch, and up the hill to her house.

"Where are you taking us?" asked Betty as well as she could, with her collar pulling at her neck.

But Lolly seemed to be in one of her frenzies of temper, rendering her deaf. She just muttered to herself. Betty's blood ran as ice. Oh help, oh help, oh help, thought Betty. She tried to look at Almira, but Lolly kept snapping them this way and that. Then, over the roaring in her ears, she thought she heard another sound, like a low-pitched rumble, and something brushed by her so closely that it made Lolly stop muttering, drop the girls, and cry out.

"GUNTHER! YOU DARNED FOOL! YOU RUN

THROUGH MY CABBAGES! GET THAT YELLER WORK OF THE MOTORCAR DEVIL OUTTA HERE!"

But the yellow car swerved around again and stopped, and out popped Grant. Betty was too stunned to move. Grant grabbed the girls from where they lay on the ground.

"Get in, get in," he whispered hurriedly.

Lolly was waving her arms wildly.

"Now you've done it, Grant Grunt! Now you is in for it! Your whole evil family is in fer it!"

But Grant stepped on the gas even before he had the doors closed and sped the car helter-skelter down the hill. When they got to the road, he shut both doors and drove on toward town.

The girls panted in the backseat. Almira rubbed her neck and finally sat up. "Stop the car," she whispered.

"It's okay, I think I can drive it for a while, if there isn't anything else on the road," said Grant worriedly. "I think we better put a little space between ourselves and Lolly."

"Stop the car," said Almira more firmly. "I'm going to be sick."

Grant stopped the car, everyone got out, and Almira threw up all over the road. Grant looked back to the house, but Lolly wasn't coming after them. The three of them stood silently for a minute, then Grant said, "Anyone for a ride?"

They climbed in again. He drove down the road until they got to the pond at the mouth of the creek. He pulled the car off into the grass.

"It ain't so hard to drive. I did a lot of damage to them cabbages trying to learn though," he said. "I guess I'm gonna be in pretty hot water over that."

They got out and went to the willow, where an old rope swing hung from a branch that jutted over the pond. They had spent many innocent carefree summer days here, swinging over the creek to the pond and dropping in. They climbed up the tree and reconnoitered.

"All in all," said Grant, "I think it would be smarter to spend this Saturday in the tree."

"What's Ma gonna think when we don't come home and the car is gone?" asked Betty. "She'll be awfully worried."

"When Lolly goes over and tells all, she'll be able to figure it out," said Grant.

So the children spent the day wading in the cold pond waters and napping in the sun, and as suppertime approached and they feared death by slow starvation, they got back into the car.

"You think . . ." said Betty. "You think I could drive it?"

"You better let me," said Grant.

"Why?" asked Betty.

"It ain't natural for womenfolk to drive things. You ain't got the same technical abilities, is all."

"I think," said Betty, "I think since I'm already a delinquent by now, I think, yes, you get outta the driver's seat, Grant Grunt. I'm gonna drive this car."

Betty sat behind the wheel. Almira and Grant cowered in the backseat. Betty knew just what to do, but when she put her foot on the gas, the car leapt forward so suddenly that she almost smashed it into a tree.

"Let me drive," said Grant. *"Please!"*

"Now you just cut that out, Grant Grunt," said Betty, concentrating on the steering wheel and the pedals. "I guess if you can ruin a field of cabbages learning how to drive the thing, I can hit a few trees."

"You put a mark on this car and you're really going to find out what trouble is," said Grant.

"I think if I just go nice and slow, I can do it," Betty muttered. When she eased the car out of the meadow and got it turned the right way up the road, Almira and Grant began to relax. The meadows and air had a pleasant end-of-day, end-of-spring feel. The sky was a lovely haze. Betty, released momentarily from her own strict moral junctures, enjoyed the delirious freedom of the fugitive. For once, nothing in the past or the future seemed very important, only this moment with the soft spring air, the quiet, contented birds calling to each other, the smell of tall grasses bending, the wonderful power of driving the car.

She took as long as she could getting to their hill, eased the car on up, and stopped when she figured it was just about where her father had left it. Then Almira ran home, and Grant and Betty sauntered up to their porch, the delirious sense of wonder encasing Betty until she heard her father's voice boom right through the window, "SHE DID WHAT?"

"You heard me, you old blasphemer, them delinquent children of yours are a blight on the potato of life."

"And you say Grant drove my car through your cabbage patch?"

"You got ears, Gunther Grunt? Listen and hear. Listen and hear."

"Well, well, well, Lolly Finnerty," they heard their father say, "you done slipped your trolley."

"See for yourself, that car of yours been gone all day. Those kids is probably halfway to Texas by now."

Grant and Betty ducked down behind the rocking chairs as Lolly waved an arm expansively out the window. They saw their parents peer through the window, Althea with a puckered frown around her eyes and Gunther looking superior and skeptical.

"I see the car parked where it derned well is always parked, Lolly," said Gunther, smiling like a crocodile.

Lolly's head shot through the window. "You'll have to take my word for it as a God-fearing woman, which you know I am, Gunther Grunt. And, Althea, I don't like to say nothin' to my own husband's sister, but you is raising that other daughter of yours like a slut."

"Well!" said Althea, twisting her skirt hem. "Well!"

"I seen with my own eyes that she was sitting in the candy store last Saturday with a *man*. I knowed she was supposed to be working, because if she weren't, you would have sent her to see Reverend Horsefeathers with us."

"Might be you were mistaken. But," Althea said, drawing herself up suddenly and letting go of her hem, "even if you weren't, even if she were having a tango down Main Street, I fail to see what business it is of yours, Lolly Finnerty. And furthermore, if Grant was taking your sons' Sunday-collection money and spending it on penny candy, perhaps you ought to speak to your own sons about it and never mind mine. *And* I fail to see, I do truly fail to see, what it is you are finding fault with Betty for."

"Your own children gallivanting in that frightful yellow car. That car has *sin* written all over it, Althea Finnerty Grunt. Sin, sin, sin. Why, crawling into that car is like aiding and abetting the work of the devil. It's handing over your immortal soul without the slightest little ole struggle."

"I heard enough," said Gunther, getting up and opening the door. "If the car were gone like you said, we might not think you was just coming all apart at the seams like I always thought you would, but as it is, you is gonna have to just drop that stuffing someplace else."

"I only have this to say for *you,* Althea," Lolly went on, lumbering absently toward the door. "You ain't never sending that girl of yours to college. Not while you're married to this no-account."

Althea drew in her breath, and Betty, peeking through the window again, could see her blinking her eyes rapidly. Garth, who had been sitting quietly under the kitchen table throughout the tirade, rose up suddenly and shouted, "You're wrong, you old bat, you old windbag!"

"Oh . . . Garth," said Althea with a trembling voice. "You oughtn't to call your elders names."

But Garth, red-faced, continued: "Betty's going to college because we know where to find Hilda's money that she hid on Uncle Herman and Uncle Willy's farm. We just have to find her diary and read where she hid it, and there will be more than enough money for college. So there. Ha."

The grownups turned and stared at Garth. Then Lolly's mouth shut with an audible clap, as if she had simply run out of strength to keep it open. She shook an admonishing finger to all in general and slammed out. Althea and Gunther and Garth followed her, their mouths agape. They watched silently until she had gone boom boom boom, all the way down the hill, and then Althea spoke. "I'll get dinner on the table," she said, and went inside.

Gunther went back in, too. Betty and Grant took this opportunity to pounce on Garth. He started to shout in surprise, but Grant put a hand over his mouth.

"You little nincompoop!" hissed Grant. "You've ruined everything. You weren't supposed to tell anyone about the money. Now we're going to have to boil you in oil."

Garth turned white.

"Oh, let him go," said Betty wearily. "Nobody pays any attention to him anyway."

Grant dropped Garth in disgust. "Pa's gonna kill you both," said Garth, unloosed. "He knows the car was gone. He asked Ma where it was."

"Well, luckily he hates Lolly more than he's mad at us," said Betty.

"I wouldn't count on it," said Grant. "I sure wish I had somewhere else to have dinner tonight. Anyhow, he can't *prove* it was us that took the car."

This Betty knew for the whistling in the wind that it was, and she and Grant crept warily in to dinner. However, Betty was, in large part, right. Gunther, who could only entertain one fury at a time, was so busy fuming about Lolly that he had forgotten about the children and the car.

"Did you see that? Ha! I got her good. I sure got her good that time. The car's gone, she says. Well, look out the window with your own eyes, I say. Hroo. And there's the car, sittin' pretty as you please. Hrunk!"

"You sure got her good, Pa," ventured Grant with a congenial, nervous little chuckle.

"I ever find that car gone again . . ." Gunther turned to him, his eyebrows beginning to grow together.

"And Garth," interjected Althea, hastily putting food on the table, "I know you were just sticking up for me, honey, but you shouldn't have talked to your Aunt Lolly that way. Especially such pointless lies! I don't know what has gotten into this family today."

Gretel came in the door just then. She looked around. "Well, did someone *die*?" she asked.

• Ten •

Monday morning when Betty came down for breakfast, her father and Gretel had already eaten and left. Garth was sitting under the table doing something indeterminate with the crumbs. Grant was eating silently with great concentration, as was his wont. This was all as usual; it was Betty's mother that worried her. She looked a bit peaked. She looked a bit pale. She was crumbling a biscuit into her coffee.

"I wouldn't drink that if I were you," said Betty.

Althea started. "Oh, Lord," she said, and dumped the coffee in the sink. "I went over to the crest of our hill—you know the part where you can see through the trees and down toward Treacle's place?"

"Yes?" said Grant, looking up.

"And her cabbage field was certainly run over. Car tracks. Just like she said. Your father isn't very fond of Lolly, or he would have paid more attention to what she said. He was so busy being mad, he forgot the cabbage part. I don't know what to say, Grant, except we'll just have to find some way to pay for those cabbages, and I can't think how to do that, except you will have to go over and see if you can't work it off. If it *did* happen that way, which I'm not saying it did. Only you know, of course. I guess what I'm asking you is to do the honorable thing, since I hope—and I've been thinking about this since Lolly's visit—I hope that, even though I had to raise you without all the advantages I may have liked, at least I give you a sense of what is right and what is not and what is honorable and what is not. And I hope you would come to the conclusion that running over someone's cabbages, especially when they're counting on eating them all winter, is hardly the honorable thing to do. If it did happen that way, and I'm not saying it did."

Grant frowned into his eggs. Betty, standing and trying to plait her froth of hair, thought how much he looked like Gunther when he did that. Why, she had never noticed how beetly his brow was nor how fuzzy his eyebrows, but they came together now like one long serpent. She fully expected him to say "hrunk," but when he spoke, all he said was that he had better get to school, and grabbing his books, he ran up to his room and back down, clomping out with a bang on the screen door that bounced it several times. Betty took her books and a piece of corn bread and ran after him. Garth tried to follow, but Althea stopped him before he even got to the door. "Garth Grunt, you haven't eaten breakfast or washed your face."

"I've got to learn to run a little faster," he muttered sadly.

Betty caught Grant just as he went over the crest of the hill. "Wait, Grant, wait. What are you going to do?"

"I'll tell you what I *ain't* going to do: I *ain't* going to go to work for that old ogre. She'll take a strip outta me if I even get near her. I got some money saved, I got three dollars and it's all I *do* got and it's all I'm likely to get now that Lolly has discovered my little business transactions with Percy and Myron. But I figure it oughta cover the damage to those old cabbages, which we wouldn't have damaged to begin with if she hadn't been intent on murder. Anyhow, I figure I don't owe her a thing, but I ain't gonna tell Ma the whole story and I ain't gonna have her bothering Ma about it anymore, so I'll give her the stupid three bucks and that'll be an end to that. I'll just leave it at her door with a note."

"Oh, Grant!" said Betty, as he went up several notches in her estimation. "I feel like I ought to give you half the money."

"You ought to give me all of it, if you ask me," said Grant grumpily. "It was your hide I was saving. Weren't me that didn't know how to spy without being found out, not to mention putting an end to a very profitable business, thank you very much, and all because you're such a great big snoop."

"I was only trying to find out how to make some money to get flowers to be Pork-Fry Queen!" wailed Betty.

"Pork-Fry Queen!" said Grant, snorting. "And look at all the trouble you caused."

"I caused? I suppose you think it's honest spending collection-plate money on candy? Anyhow, if I had any money I'd give it to you, but then if I had any money I wouldn't have followed you in the first place."

"Well, you haven't got any money and I haven't got any money anymore, so now the only one who is gonna have any money is Lolly. So where does that get us?"

Betty figured there wasn't much point trying to answer that, and besides, they were approaching Lolly's farmhouse. Just as they reached the porch and Grant started to write a message to Lolly on a piece of notebook paper, they heard the Finnertys' pickup truck start. It rumbled around from the back of the house. They stood frozen until Lolly, who was at the wheel, with Myron, Percy, and Uncle Treacle in the back, pulled to a stop and roared, *"You again!* You handmaidens of Satan!"

"I beg your pardon?" said Betty.

"What are you doing on my land? I'll fry you alive, I'll stake you to the fence and leave you for the ants, I'll . . ."

"We're giving you some money for your cabbages, is all, Lolly, and then you'll never see us again. Not if we see you first," said Grant in a clear voice, but Betty noticed his legs were shaking almost as violently as her own.

"I'll . . . How much money you say, boy?"

"Three dollars. In nickels mostly," said Grant, inching forward toward the truck, as though he expected Lolly to spring out at any moment.

"Bring it here, offer it up, boy, offer it up," hollered Lolly.

So Grant advanced, slowly and smoothly, the way you approach a wild beast. Lolly reached a long, fat arm out of the truck and snatched the money from his hand, and, stepping on the gas, roared out the drive and on down the hill to the road.

Grant sat down where he was, unmindful of the dust from Lolly's truck, and wiped his forehead.

Betty came and stood over him, watching the truck wind down the hill and away through the rolling road below.

"Well, that's done, at least," she said.

Grant got up slowly and dusted off his pants, went back to the porch, picked up his books, and started slowly along the road for school. Betty walked silently beside him.

Presently he said, "I wonder where they was going?"

"What do you mean?" asked Betty.

"Why weren't Myron and Percy going to school? And how come Uncle Treacle was in the back of the truck? You know Lolly never uses that truck except to cart him around."

"Probably found another preacher who heals folks," said Betty.

"I guess," said Grant.

"Listen, Grant, we've got to get Pa to drive us back to Willy and Herman's this Sunday. Next Monday I have to have the money in to be the Pork-Fry Queen, or else it's gonna be Janine Woodrow."

"What do I care if Janine Woodrow is the Pork-Fry Queen? Girls set store by the stupidest things. You really want to get hauled onto a field on top of a side of ribs?"

"If you don't see the glory of it, I can't possibly explain. Anyhow, if we find the money, we're splitting it three ways, and then I can give you three dollars of my share to pay you back for the three dollars you had to give Aunt Lolly. But suppose Mac and Sam get there first? They've already started digging, haven't they?"

"Oh, all right. But isn't it going to look kind of peculiar, us always wanting to go to Uncle Willy and Uncle Herman's?"

"You just have to think of a good reason. We'll work on them at suppertime, okay?" said Betty as they approached her school.

"Jeez, to think I'd be in cahoots with a girl, and my own sister at that," said Grant, and ran on ahead to his school.

But, thought Betty, he didn't say no.

She hung around the door to the school until she saw Garth approach, and she told him about their plan.

"But this time," she said, leveling him a look, "you must keep your mouth shut."

Garth nodded, and the bell rang.

That night at dinner, over, ironically, pork chops, Betty said in her sweetest tones, "Pa, I really can't wait to go on a drive this Sunday."

"Hrunk," said Gunther.

"It's just about the high point of the week, wouldn't you say, Grant?"

"Yeah, it's okay," said Grant. She kicked him. "I like it. It's peachy!"

"The longer the ride, the better, I'd say. I bet Uncle Herman and Uncle Willy would love to get a look at the car again," said Betty.

Gunther said nothing, but took all his peas and piled them on top of a hill of mashed potatoes, mixed them up, and began to systematically shove them into his mouth.

"Why, what an ingenious way to eat peas!" chirped Betty.

Gunther stopped eating, his brows pulled together in a frown of suspicion.

"I believe I'll eat my own that way," she said quickly, mixing her peas and potatoes into one disgusting mass and shoveling them in at such a great rate that it caused her finally—as her father frowned at her, unable to figure out whether or not he was being mocked—to choke on a pea and cough the whole matter across the table in an appalling white and green froth.

"Oh, Jesus Christ!" said Grant, wiping peas off his sleeves.

"Grant Grunt, you watch your language. Betty, dear, are you quite all right? Perhaps," said their mother, getting a wet cloth and sponging off the various members of the family, "you ought to slow down a little, dear."

Betty, her face still red and her eyes glazed, nodded but continued coughing. Everyone stopped eating and looked at her in fascination. Finally, with a stray cough here and there and her color subsiding, she dabbed at her mouth in a ladylike way, whispered hoarsely, "Excuse me," and went back to eating her dinner.

Gunther, convinced he hadn't been mocked, resumed eating, oblivious to the mashed potatoes stuck to his eyebrows. Garth looked around and decided he had better take matters in hand.

"We want to go to Uncle Willy and Uncle Herman's Sunday," he said.

Betty clutched her head. He was incorrigible!

"Going to town," said Gunther. "Wanna look in the hardware-store window. Never do get a chance to do that. Hrunk."

"Window shopping," said Althea, and her eyes took on a dreamy look, and she forgot to ask how they would be getting to town.

"But WE WANT TO GO TO WILLY AND HERMAN'S!" said Garth.

"You can leave the table!" roared Gunther.

And that was the end of the discussion.

Sunday, dressed in their best clothes and begloved and behatted, the Grunts began the slow drive into town. Gunther was a reasonably good driver by now, it was a soft spring day full of promise, and Betty was full of hope. In town Gunther parked carefully and then, like a man of means, stood proudly outside the car, wiping the occasional spot off it, looking as though he hoped someone he knew would happen by to see him standing by his yellow car, but equally content to show it off to strangers.

"Now, children," said Althea, "I'm going to have a peek in the shop windows, and your father wants to look at the hardware store. If there's anything you'd like to see, I suggest you do it now and we'll meet you back here in an hour."

Gretel elected to window-shop with Althea. As soon as the grownups had departed, Betty grabbed Garth and Grant.

"Come on, this is our chance," she said.

"Our chance for what?" snorted Grant.

"The road to Herman and Willy's farm is just past the corner. Let's go put our thumbs out. I saw that man doing it on our way here. You put your thumb out, and someone gives you a ride."

"Have you gone completely crazy?" asked Grant.

"I figure we can get there in, oh, say we get a ride right away, fifteen minutes. Then we look in the diary, find out exactly where the money is, dig it up, and get Uncle Willy to give us a ride back to town. And the whole thing takes two hours, tops."

"We're supposed to meet them back at the car in an hour," pointed out Grant.

"Well, they'll have to wait for us. What else are

• 127 •

they going to do? They'd never leave without us."

"Can you imagine how mad Pa will be after an hour of waiting?"

"We'll have to chance it," said Betty.

"Chance it so you can become the Pork-Fry Queen? I don't think so, no sirree, not on a bet, not this boy," said Grant, leaning against the side of the building and laughing.

"I'll go with you," said Garth, looking like a faithful puppy.

"Good. If we find the money, we'll split it two ways," said Betty. "Though, of course, Grant, I will give you the money I owe you."

"Now just a cotton-pickin' minute," said Grant. "You call that fair?"

"No, it's not fair, and it's not fair that just because Janine Woodrow has a father who happens to own some big department store she can be Pork-Fry Queen just any old time she likes. Just any old time she likes." And Betty sat down on the curb and burst into tears.

Betty, in the throes of despair, was not a pretty sight. Her skin turned red and blotchy, not just her face but her neck as well, and her frizzy hair seemed suddenly frizzier, as though the static electricity of her mood had affected it somehow. Her nose ran and her eyes swelled to piggy blindness. Grant, looking at her, thought she was a sight, all right. He marveled that she could ever have been elected to queen of anything but the toad ball, and the fact that she had and couldn't seize the chance suddenly seemed kind of pathetic.

"Oh heck," he said. "I still don't know why you want to be some old Pork-Fry Queen. I mean, I could understand why you might want to go to college someday, but this Pork-Fry-Queen stuff just seems dumb to me. Still, I guess you shouldn't spit on miracles, and believe me, you don't want to know what I mean by that. I better go along and protect my investment, so let's go."

The children ran down Main Street as fast as they could and kept running down the road to their uncles', stopping only to put out their thumbs when they heard a car coming. But cars were few and far between and, oddly enough, not interested in picking them up, although they tried their best to look pleasant but desperate. Finally, a farmer stopped and let them ride in the back of his truck, but he seemed extremely disapproving which bothered Betty, who compensated by whispering to her brothers to appear upright, until they told her to shut up. When he pulled in front of Willy and Herman's farm, they were sweaty and covered in chicken feathers. They thanked him, and he gave them a short grunt and drove on.

Uncle Willy and Uncle Herman could be seen

out in the fields, so Grant and Betty ran into the library to search for the diary while Garth ran down to tell their uncles what they were up to.

"Where is it? Where is it?" said Betty impatiently. She was so excited at finally having her dollar to be Pork-Fry Queen that a queer flush was on her face, and she didn't care if her father was so angry that he exploded.

Betty and Grant peered up one shelf and down the next. When they had finished the lower shelves, which mostly seemed to be books in German, and had pulled chairs over to begin the top shelves, Garth appeared with Uncle Herman beside him.

"Ahem," he cleared his throat. "I think I got what you want," he said, not daring to look at them, and went over to the desk and pulled out Hilda's diary. "I gotta go back to the fields," he muttered, and slunk out.

Garth and Grant both reached to grab it, but Betty slapped them away.

"Who," she roared, "in this family reads the best?"

"You do," they said.

"And who," she roared, "in this family reads the fastest?"

"Well, get on with it, then," said Grant.

So Betty curled up in a wing chair and began frantically skimming the pages. There seemed to be a lot about the cows' little antics. Betty had no idea that a cow could have so much personality. Today, she read, was an important day.

"Listen, boys, I think I have it!" she said. The three stopped breathing.

" 'Today,' " read Betty, " 'Bessie ate a bug.' "

"Oh, you're kidding. She doesn't say that," said Grant.

"Yes, she does. I swear to you," said Betty.

"Well, hurry up, and don't read out loud to us until you're sure you have it," said Grant.

Garth began to tap his foot furiously on the floor. Tap, tap, tap, tap, tap, tap, tap, tap.

"Stop it!" shouted Betty. "Stop it! I can't read when you're tapping. I just keep reading the same sentence over and over and over."

"Go outside and play," said Grant, giving Garth a shove.

"I wanna be here, too!" said Garth, who stopped tapping and began to crack his knuckles. Crack, crack, crack, crack, crack, crack, crack.

"I'll go outside with you," barked Grant. "Come on, read, read," he shouted at Betty, and led Garth outside.

Betty read. She read as fast as she could. She willed herself to read faster, but it was a long diary, Aunt Hilda's tiny spiderlike handwriting was hard to read, and Betty was afraid of skimming over the important part. But as page after page went by with only farm reports and Bessie's incredibly overinflated antics, Betty began to despair and wonder if perhaps there had never been any money to begin with. Maybe Willy and Herman had made up the story. Maybe they had been mistaken. And now it was getting to the end of the diary. She could see Janine Woodrow riding in glory on a side of pork, when, suddenly, there it was, large as life, spelled out in a beautiful clear print:

TODAY I HID THE MONEY.

"Grant," she called through the open window, dancing around the chair deliriously, "Grant, Garth, come in! I've FOUND IT!"

· Eleven ·

Garth and Grant scrambled in. They were in such a hurry to get into the house that they tried to push through the partially open window, which was held up by a rickety stick. As they shoved each other, the stick fell out and the window came crashing down on their middles, causing them to scream and Betty, who was in a state of high excitement, to scream louder than both of them put together and to go quite purple. When they had all calmed down a fraction, it was the work of a moment for Betty to open the window and the boys to roll onto the floor, where they fell into a tangled pile just as Herman walked in.

"I been thinkin'," he said, shuffling around the room. "Your folks know you're here?"

"No," said the children.

"Read it," said Grant, barely taking note of Herman.

"How'd you get here?" asked Herman.

"Hitchhiked from town," said Betty. "I *can't* read it. It's in German."

"Then, how do you know it's about the money?" yelled Grant.

"Because it says in English, 'This is where I hid the money.' Then after that, it's in German."

"But we don't read German," whined Garth, as though the book was taking unfair advantage of them.

"What are we going to do?" wailed Betty.

"Wait a second, let me think," said Grant, pressing his hands to his head as though trying to squeeze out a thought. *"You* read German, don't you?" he asked Herman.

"Yes," said Herman, looking at the ceiling. "Mutter taught us German."

"Well, can't you read it to us and tell us what it means?"

"I could. Don't have to, though. I already translated it once."

"You know where the money is?" yelled Grant. "You've known all along where the money is?"

"Don't know where the money is, no. If I knew

that, I would have told Garth. Now wait a second here, I think that's why Sam and Mac keep coming back to dig up the pasture. Couldn't make no sense of it before. I keep sending them home, and they keep coming back and digging. Derndest thing, I thought."

"WHAT DOES THE GERMAN MEAN?" screamed Betty. Let Sam and Mac dig. She and Grant and Garth were going to get the money.

"It says under the potato bin in the root cellar. Where's Althea anyhow?" asked Uncle Herman, looking troubled, but the children leapt up before the sentence was out of his mouth.

Down the hill they flew to a little knoll with a door in it, which was the root cellar. Inside, in the cool dimness, they found the potato bin.

"What are we going to do with all these potatoes?" asked Grant, staring dispiritedly at the ton of them sitting in the big wooden bin.

"Take them out," said Betty.

"And do what with them?"

"Throw them on the ground. For heaven's sake, they're stored in dirt, it's not like they're going to get dirty or bruised or something."

So the children threw them out the door over their shoulders as quickly as they could. Half an hour later, there were still piles of potatoes, and the children's shoulders were stiff and sore.

"You can see why I'd rather be a catcher than a

pitcher, can't you, Grant? Can't you, Grant? Huh, can't you?" asked Garth in an exasperating way.

"Yes!" yelled Grant, who was dirty and tired and getting nervous about being gone for so long. "If you just shut up, you can be the baseball, for all I care."

The children continued to work, throwing potatoes out as fast as they could. Finally when there was a mountain of potatoes outside the door and the children were covered in grime from head to foot, they lifted the potato bin and fell onto their knees to dig the soft earth. Down, down they dug until finally they struck metal.

"Oh my GOSH. GOLD!" yelled Betty, who wasn't thinking clearly and collapsed in a faint, unable to summon the strength to sit up.

Garth continued doggedly and was the first to yank it out. "No, no, it's a baking-powder can."

"A BAKING-POWDER CAN!" shouted Betty.

"Shut up and open it," yelled Grant, grabbing it from Garth and opening it himself.

It was empty.

The children's mouths hung open. They stared at each other.

"Why would someone bury an empty baking-powder can?" asked Betty.

"Maybe there's something else buried," said Garth, and resumed digging.

"Wait a second," said Grant. "There's something

I don't understand. How come Uncle Herman knew there was something in German in the diary and what it was?"

A shadow loomed in the doorway. "WHAT IN TARNATION ARE YOU CHILDREN DOING HERE?" came a voice. The children leapt up. There stood their parents and Gretel. Behind them stood Uncle Herman and Uncle Willy.

"How did you know we were here?" asked Grant in a squeaky voice.

"Mothers," said Althea, "know everything. Children, get in the car."

"No one gets in the car looking like that," said their father. "Serve you right if I made you walk home."

The children glanced at each other. Their hands were dirt-encrusted, their faces were gloomy and smudged, and their best clothes were a shambles.

"Herman and Willy, would you mind if I took the children in and washed them?" asked Althea.

"Go ahead," said Willy, gazing at the potatoes.

"What the *heck* you children doing here?" roared Gunther again.

"Popular place," said Willy.

"Popular place," said Herman. "Treacle and Lolly come through."

"They took out all our potatoes, too," said Willy.

"Met their sons for the first time," said Herman.

"Percy," said Willy.

"Myron," said Herman.

Betty looked at Grant. Grant looked at Betty.

"Did you translate the diary for them?" asked Grant. "Didn't you know what they were up to?"

"Weren't really none of our business," said Willy.

"It's your farm!" said Grant.

"She said weren't none of our business," said Herman.

"You mean Lolly?" asked Grant. "She would. But didn't you . . ." he began, but Althea interposed.

"Now children, I will not have you talking to your uncles that way. I never did in my whole entire days. You get up to that bathroom right now and wash yourselves and make yourselves presentable. To think of the worry you could have caused if I wasn't, as usual, right."

"What the *heck* were you children doing here?" roared Gunther, no doubt hoping someone would answer him this time.

"Oh, Gunther, it was just one of their silly games. I don't know what Lolly wanted, but I'm sure she wouldn't believe anymore than we did that Hilda was ever able to get ahold of any money. She wasn't herself toward the end, and maybe she really did believe she was rich, but no one else did," said Althea, herding the disheartened crew up to the house.

"Sam and Mac have been digging for it," said

Garth. Betty and Grant groaned. Would he never learn to keep quiet?

"Oh, for heaven's sake, I don't think any of you have the sense you were born with. All this fuss and trouble about something that never was. We're going to be late for church if we don't hurry, and I really don't know what the reverend will say about that."

The children ran into the house and washed themselves as best they could. Their clothes were still fairly grimy, but there was nothing they could do about it.

"Lolly's got it, sure as shooting," said Grant as they washed their hands and faces. "But it's just as well Ma doesn't believe in it. I'm all for breaking into their house and stealing it right back."

"What do you mean stealing it back?" asked Betty. "It's not our money either."

"It is, too. Herman said it was Garth's if he found it," said Grant.

"Couldn't we just explain things to her?" said Betty.

"To Lolly?" said Grant, looking incredulous.

"All right," said Betty, hope springing eternal. "Let's get it."

"In the middle of the night," put in Garth.

"Of course, in the middle of the night," said Grant.

"We could bind and gag Lolly just for the fun of it," said Garth.

"Settle down," said Betty and Grant together.

"I think," said Grant, "that if you need that dollar tomorrow, we had better do it tonight."

"It's our last chance," agreed Betty.

The car ride home was quiet. The children dared not say anything to their father, who turned slowly around every so often and gave them a look and a reproving "hrunk." Gretel seemed nervous and wrapped in her own thoughts, as she had been all day. She stared out the window and sighed periodically, which Betty would have considered interesting if she hadn't been so focused on her own immediate needs.

After church the children went to bed right away. When the grownups had been to bed long enough for the children to be sure they were sleeping, Betty crept into the boys' room and the three children climbed out onto the slanting roof, slid carefully to the edge, hung by their hands until their feet touched the porch railing, teetered unsteadily on that, and jumped to the ground below. They could have sneaked down the hall stairs, but what would have been the fun of that?

Down the hill they went, dodging in and out of the trees in case someone was watching, darting from shadow to shadow, and, finally, through the cabbage fields, toward the house, and—quietly, quietly, with stealth galore—into the enemy camp, through their parlor, and into their kitchen.

"Where do we look first?" hissed Grant. This being the first thing anyone had said, it so startled Garth that he fell backward and, most unfortunately, right into stacks and stacks of canning. Thousands, hundreds of thousands of jars fell by the sound of it, this way and that. They rolled. They crashed. They broke. It was artillery fire. It was thunder. It was the voice of doom. The children stood breathless, their adrenaline gathering and shooting off into their blood, preparing them to fly out the door. Indeed, Betty's feet were already beginning to gravitate there, when Grant pulled her back by the sleeve.

"Listen," he whispered.

They listened.

"I don't hear anything," said Betty, barely able to hear her own whisper over the pounding of her heart.

"Exactly," said Grant, and flipped on a light.

"Turn that off," hissed Betty.

"Are you kidding?" said Grant in a normal voice. He went over to the kitchen window and looked out back. "No one's here. We made enough noise to bring even Treacle to his feet. Truck's gone. They've taken a powder."

"The old twenty-three skiddoo," said Garth in awe.

"Cheezed it," said Grant.

Betty looked from one to the other, trying to absorb this. Then she let out a wail like a banshee having a spinal puncture.

"NOW I'LL NEVER BE PORK-FRY QUEEN!"

· Twelve ·

Betty dreaded the next day at school. She considered not going at all, but she knew that even if she would never be queen of anything, she had to hold on to the chance that someday she would go to college. It was all she had left. So she trudged to school, answered as many questions as she could correctly, and tried to look earnest, pleasant, morally upright, intelligent, and gosh darn fun to boot, but after recess Miss Fenster called her in anyway.

"I've . . . I've decided I don't want to be Pork-Fry Queen," she said in low tones. "The fact is, I'm going to be pretty busy studying for college and all."

Miss Fenster smirked. "I'm sorry to hear that. Then I guess I will just have to ask Janine to do the honors."

"Maybe," said Betty, holding out hope to the last, "Janine won't have a dollar."

Miss Fenster pulled a dollar out of her pocket. "This is Janine's dollar. I have been holding it in escrow."

Betty made a mental note to look up "escrow"— such was her mettle that in her darkest hour she was ready to forge on, never to lose sight of her long-range goals, ever ready to improve herself. Someday, she thought, looking at Miss Fenster's retreating back, I will be a great, world-famous something, and I will come back to this little two-bit burg and I will squish you like a bug.

Miss Fenster made the announcement right before school let out. Janine Woodrow turned in her seat and gave Betty a long sympathetic look. Almira rolled her eyes. After school, she ran up and gave Betty's arm a squeeze.

"You were magnificent," she said as they walked slowly home from school. "The way you didn't cry in front of everybody or anything. Gosh, I would have bawled my eyes out, it was so humiliating."

"You are not making me feel better," said Betty coldly.

"Oh, well, look at it this way, she's just gonna get pork fat all over her best dress. Who wants to ride into a field on a side of ribs? It's ridiculous really, if you think about it."

"Ludicrous," said Betty.

"Anyhow, I wouldn't even *go* to the Pork-Fry Festival now if I were you. My mother says it's about time they stop asking kids for money for things. They know no one's got any. She says your mother ought to march in and ask just what kind of a democracy we live in, anyway."

"I'm afraid my mother has bigger fish to fry," said Betty.

When they got to Betty's hill, Almira waved goodbye and started off down the valley to her house. Betty looked up the hill to Lolly's, but there was still no sign of life. She trudged up to her own house and said hello to her mother, grabbed a handful of hermit cookies, went to sit in her apple tree, and, there, finally by herself, cried until her insides were squeezed dry. Then she dried her eyes, fanned her face, and, hoping she didn't look as though she had been crying, went in to dinner.

No one said much of anything at dinner. She guessed Grant and Garth were thinking of their own disappointments. Their father looked tired and sour. Their mother was busy hanging laundry inside the house as it started to rain outside. Gretel came home looking more worried than usual, and Betty realized that it had been a long time since she had regaled them with slices of life. The rain pit-patted cozily on the roof of the house, but Betty's heart was as stone, unable to get any comfort from the storm.

She wondered if her family was so obtuse that they didn't even realize what a bad day she had had. Finally, lying in bed that night staring at the ceiling, she could contain herself no more.

"I'm not going to be the Pork-Fry Queen," she said to Gretel, who was sitting at the vanity, staring at herself. "I couldn't come up with the dollar for flowers, so Janine Woodrow is going to be the Pork-Fry Queen."

She didn't know what she expected Gretel to say, but she certainly hadn't expected her to erupt in hysterical sobs, throw herself into her closet, and beat the floor with her fists.

"Oh, now, stop that!" said Betty. "Even *I* didn't do that." She was miffed. This was, when it came down to it, *her* tragedy. She always did think Gretel had a peculiar streak.

"I'm going to get married," said Gretel, sobbing and still pounding the floor.

"Don't you want to get married?" asked Betty, forgetting for a moment about being the Pork-Fry Queen.

"Of course I want to get married, you fool," spat Gretel, emerging red-eyed from the closet. "I'm going to marry Clarence. He thinks my family is living in Italy. He thinks I took the job at the bus station for a lark, to get a slice of life. We're getting married on Sunday, and I told him my family is so rich that even though they can't be there, they plan to give us a glorious wedding present instead of a big wedding."

"Oh Gretel, for heaven's sake," said Betty. Gretel really was just too stupid. "Why don't you tell him the truth?"

"Not ever," said Gretel, howling. "Not ever."

"Well, are you never going to see us, is that it?" asked Betty. "You're just going to marry this Mr. Fancypants and run away and never see us again?" Betty was thunderstruck at this idea. Didn't Gretel love them?

"Oh, of course, someday, someday I'll tell him. Someday when I'm more sure of things. But I can't do it now. He'll just think I'm a big liar."

"You *are* a big liar, Gretel," said Betty consolingly.

"I know it," said Gretel tearfully. "What am I going to do? He is expecting my family to come up with a wonderful wedding present."

"Why don't you tell him your family disapproves of you marrying so young and has disowned you?"

"I can't. I've already told him my family is happy for us but can't be here. It's too late to be disowned."

"Oh Gretel, if you're going to be a big liar, you're going to have to at least develop a little finesse.

What are you going to tell Ma and Pa? Their feelings are going to be so hurt. How are you going to explain that you won't let your husband know about them because you're ashamed of them?"

"It's just gonna have to be, Betty. It's just gonna have to be. Someday you'll understand. Someday you'll meet someone like Clarence, and you won't care about anything else."

"Well, I hope I have the sense to fall in love with someone who doesn't care if I'm poor. Anyhow, Gretel, everyone is poor these days."

"Clarence isn't. And besides, Betty, you think if it weren't a depression we wouldn't be poor? Our folks are always gonna be poor. We're just plain shiftless, trash."

"Gretel Grunt, we are no such thing. What about Ma and her love of music? What about me and my superior intellect? Someday I'm going to college, and then make a good living and send my children to college. You ought to think about going to college, too, Gretel, and making something of yourself."

"I don't want to go to college," Gretel said. "I only want Clarence." And she cried out his name as though her heart would break.

Betty thought about this. It had never occurred to her that Gretel might want something in the same way that she wanted to be the Pork-Fry

Queen. She wondered if her mother wanted something for herself this way. She wondered if that was the way her father felt about the yellow car. She began to wonder if everyone didn't have something, something special that they wanted. She had always assumed she was the only person in the family with great longing. But perhaps everybody wanted something special, and perhaps it wasn't the something that was important. Maybe it was the wanting. She snuggled deeper into bed and thought about it some more.

"Gretel," she whispered finally, "Gretel, go to sleep. Maybe there's something we can do to solve this."

"Ha," sobbed Gretel hysterically, and continued in a limp pool to cry into the night.

Betty thought. She thought all the next day, and after dinner she went outside and sat next to her father, who was rocking on the porch, and talked to him. She talked for a long time, and he rocked and said "hrunk" and "hroo" and nodded his head, and Betty went to bed unsure how much he had listened or understood.

The next day, when she got home, the yellow car was gone. Althea was in the rocker on the porch, baskets of laundry unwashed at her feet. Betty sat down next to her.

"Did Pa give the car to Gretel?" asked Betty.

"He did," said Althea, looking down the valley. "I hope we see her again."

"Oh, I guess someday she'll tell him about us," said Betty. "She can't keep us a secret forever. What did Pa say?"

"He said he believed in hard work. He's a man who worked hard all his life, you know, Betty, and you shouldn't never undervalue that. He said it's important to work hard, stand tall, tell the truth, and go to church, but sometimes you just have to drive away."

"What did Gretel say?" asked Betty.

"Nothing," said Althea, her eyes following the road as though she could still see the back of the yellow car driving away. She sighed and got up. "I got the queerest telegram from Lolly. She wants us to sell their farm and send them the money. She and Treacle bought a house in Texas. Texas!"

"So that's what Lolly did with it!" yelled Betty.

"What?" asked Althea.

"Nothing," said Betty.

"Come on in and help me make a pie," said Althea. "I can't get myself to work today for some reason."

Betty peeled apples while Althea made a biscuit crust. She measured the flour, sugar, lard, and salt. Then, as she added the final ingredient, a funny look came into her eyes. She put in the last of the baking powder, lifted the can, and shook it upside down. Betty caught her eye, and they beamed at each other.

"Why, looky here, Betty," she said.

"My oh my," said Betty. "What you got there?"

"An empty baking-powder can," said Althea, and they put it gently, secretly away.